# THE SPIDER:
## LEGIONS OF THE ACCURSED LIGHT

THE **MASTER** OF **MEN!**

# SPIDER®

# LEGIONS OF THE ACCURSED LIGHT

*By Grant Stockbridge*

STEEGER BOOKS • 2021

PUBLISHING HISTORY

"Legions of the Accursed Light" originally appeared in the January 1938 (Vol. 13, No.
4) issue of *The Spider* magazine. Copyright 2021 by Argosy Communications, Inc.
All rights reserved.

# CHAPTER 1
## EYE OF FLAME

FOR MANY months, the truth has been suppressed. Even Richard Wentworth thought that course wisest at the time, and so concurred with the order of certain powerful governments which dreaded lest the people, learning the facts, go mad with fear! But because of those things which have happened recently, in which Wentworth—alone perhaps of all men—read the real significance, the ban has been lifted. Now, the truth *must be told!*

It seems that the Terror is not dead, or, if that dread slaughterer of human beings has succumbed, his awful secret lives after him—the secret of the Eye of Flame! It is true that men manufacture explanations of things they cannot understand, and this is why, for a time, the truth behind certain awful happenings in the Far East escaped detection. It was Wentworth who pointed out the possible significance of the fires that swept Tientsin and killed their thousands; and of the Chinese army that marched, chanting, into battle and vanished. Which is to say that nothing of those men was ever found again... nothing recognizable.

You, who read this, did not know that such things happened here in America, too, a few months ago....

It is difficult to trace the beginnings of that slaughter of which the world knew so little. Wentworth, himself, was in Schermerhorn, an industrial city in western New York, when first he saw

Suddenly, like a flash from hell, itself, the death-ray struck into the ranks of the law!

the fearful workings of the Eye of Flame. In that city, two men had died strangely and, as it developed, rather terribly, though no one then suspected—no one save that keen young madman, Horatio Smithers....

BUT LET us begin with the night that Horatio Smithers carried the message to Richard Wentworth. For several months, there had been no dangerous stirrings in the underworld other than the usual round of petty crime. Wentworth, who had dedicated his life to warfare against criminal cohorts, had thrown himself into a round of gaiety with his fiancée, Nita van Sloan.

Tonight, a bitterly cold evening near the fag end of January, they had attended the opening of a famous dramatist's play and were going on, afterward, to a dinner for the cast.

Just inside the plate-glass doors of the lobby, Wentworth and Nita van Sloan stood chatting and laughing with friends. Outside, the wind whooped and brawled, for an icy gale out of the north had made wind tunnels of New York's canyon streets. Men clutched at their silk hats and women drew their fur cloaks tightly about them against the rowdy tussling of the storm. And then, through the packed traffic of the street, Wentworth's sleek, gleaming Daimler purred its way to the curb.

It was Nita who first saw the incredible thing. Her silvery laughter broke in mid-note, and Wentworth, noting the sudden widening of her eyes, felt once more the familiar chill tightening of his scalp, the sharp prod of imminent danger, quiescent these many months. With a lithe movement that indicated the alert strength of his body, he whirled toward the doors. Instantly, there flashed across his mind the fact that he carried no gun beneath his evening dress. There were weapons in the car, of course, but....

"Good lord!" he whispered. "Of all the fool—"

He went striding through the plate-glass doors. The wind knifed at him, tightened his eyes with cold, but his glance remained keen as he swept the street, watchfully. His stare came back to the man who ran beside the Daimler, as it came to rest beside the curb. Despite the zero temperature, the man wore no coat or hat—wore not even a vest. His left hand gripped the handle of the Daimler's door and, as Wentworth darted toward him, he saw that a handcuff glinted about his wrist. He was manacled to the door!

Even in that moment of surprise, Wentworth's keen brain was conning the situation. Once more, his eyes swept the street. Before this, ambitious criminals intent on underworld domination had launched their campaigns for leadership by attacks on him. It was not that they knew his secret identity—that, as the grim, black-cloaked Spider, he dealt out a swift and deadly justice—but Wentworth had fought them in his own right also, and with a terrible efficiency. It was possible this bizarre trick was a bait to draw him into the open alone where hungry guns could blaze upon him. Yet, Wentworth did not hesitate.

The man handcuffed to his car was peering about him, groggy with cold. His face was blue with it, and shudders swept over his body. Then he saw Wentworth and, strangely, smiled. It was twisted, but authentic, that smile. It was eager and… pleading. Wentworth was aware of that even as he swept up to the man.

"Thank G-god!" the man chattered up at him. "They wouldn't l-let me see you until t-tomorrow, and it can't wait! You've g-g-got to help…."

He slumped down and, behind him as he fell, a silvery streak sprang out clearly against the glossy black of the car's door. Almost before his ears registered the sound of a pistol shot, Wentworth's eyes identified that silvery streak as the mark made by a glancing bullet—and spotted the direction from which it came.

He was already in action. One hand whipped open the rear door of the car, interposed its bullet-proof metal between them-

selves and the gun. His arm scooped
under the sagging body, and his right
hand closed on the handle of the
front door to which the handcuff was
fastened.

The roar of the gun blended with
the thud of lead against the interposed
shield of the door. Wentworth heard them dimly, just as he knew
that his turbaned chauffeur, Ram Singh, had thrust head and
shoulder out of the far window and was returning the fire. Men
and women were shouting. All his attention and strength was
concentrated on the door handle.

With a quick shift of weight and leverage, Wentworth applied
an explosive concentration of strength on the task. There was a
snap of metal, and the handle spun free, came loose in his hand.
Instantly, he heaved the man into the rear of the limousine, and
flung in behind. From a compartment, he snatched a .45 caliber
automatic and methodically jacked a cartridge into the chamber
before his eyes sought out the assassin.

BETWEEN WENTWORTH'S brows was a sharp crease
of concentration, as he deliberately opened a narrow gun-port
in the rear window. Instantly, he spotted his target. The gunman
was leaning from a second-floor window in the building next
to the theater. Even as Wentworth's eyes fell on him, the man
started to draw back. Head and body vanished, but he was
supporting his weight by an arm and hand braced on the sill.
Before he could shift balance and withdraw, Wentworth's automatic crashed once.

The blast was deafening in the narrow confines of the car, and Wentworth swore softly. He was shooting left-handed, his right still numb from the force he had exerted to break the door handle free, standing straddle-legged over the body of the unconscious man. But his eye had been true. He saw the arm of the assassin battered aside with the quarter-ton impact of his bullet, saw it flop limply, broken at the elbow. The assassin's head and shoulders popped out the window. His scream came to Wentworth, thin and muted by the thick sides of the car. Then the man was falling. His arms and legs scrambled wildly. His head struck the concrete first. Wentworth thumbed the safety on his automatic, and thrust it into his belt.

That was Wentworth's introduction to Horatio Smithers, though it was an hour later, in his unique home east off Sutton Place, before he knew the name of the man who had handcuffed himself to the door of the Daimler. For that, it developed was what he had done.

SINCE THE shooting had been futile, not even wounding Smithers, Wentworth's Sikh chauffeur, Ram Singh, was inclined to grin about the affair.

*"Wah, sahib,"* he exclaimed with a flash of white teeth behind his thick beard, "the man is a fool! He remained near the *sahib's* car until thy servant threatened to separate him from his ears. He trembled with fear then, and ran away. When next thy servant saw him, he was without his coat. He ran up to the *sahib's* car and chained himself to the door.

" 'Now!' he cried at thy servant, 'you cannot frighten me away. If you don't let me inside the car and let me wait for Mr. Wentworth, I will freeze to death. And it will be on your head!" Then he threw the key of the handcuffs far away!" The Sikh grinned.

"Now, if a fool wishes to freeze himself to death, surely it is no part of wise men to interfere. And he is a coward, since he needed chains to hold himself there against thy servant's threats!"

A slight answering smile stirred Wentworth's chiseled lips, but it was grim. "Cowards are of many kinds, O mighty Ram Singh," he said quietly. "Some men might say that thou wast afraid to permit this small, unarmed man to sit beside thee in the car. They would lie, of course, my mighty Ram Singh."

Ram Singh's great hands knotted. "Now, by the belly of the evil Kali!" he cried harshly.

Wentworth's voice sliced through his incisively, "Was it thus I treated thy people when they needed help?"

For a moment, the giant Sikh still trembled with rage. It left him suddenly. His salaam was humble. "My turban is at thy feet, master," he said.

Wentworth dismissed him curtly, went striding to the room where a doctor bent over Smithers' bed, and Nita van Sloan walked beside him.

"Oh, Dick, that was unkind," she protested. "Ram Singh will sulk for a week. And, after all, you can't argue with an Oriental's sense of humor."

Wentworth's frown refused to lift. "This man came to me for help, and he was turned away," he said shortly. "He persisted, and my servant almost caused him to lose his life. His methods were perhaps foolish, but the point is he succeeded. How about it, Doctor Griggs?"

Griggs shrugged his heavy shoulders, more suited to a wrestler than a famous surgeon. "No wounds," he said curtly. "Exposure. Exhaustion. I'd like to wring Ram Singh's neck." He jerked his square-cut head with its bristling red hair, shot out his jaw pugnaciously.

"You have my full permission to try," Wentworth grinned. "I want to talk to this man. *Now.*"

Nita's hand was on Wentworth's arm, her violet eyes searching his profile. There was a grimness and urgency there, she recognized. Perhaps, inwardly, she felt a twinge of regret. These last few months had been theirs to share, and such peace came so rarely. She knew all Wentworth's secrets, had fought beside him times without number against the criminal hordes. She had accepted his dictum that, while the Spider still must creep through perilous nights—while the law might strike him down at any hour for his crimes of justice—they could never marry. Now, once more danger lay ahead. Her intuition seconded her logic in that thought. Only, not even Nita, who had shared so many of his perils, could guess the full horror of what lay before them.

Wentworth's hand closed over hers. Doubtless, he guessed the tenor of her thoughts, and his next words confirmed her fears.

"Better arrange to occupy your suite here, dear," he said quietly.

Wentworth's home, erected partly on filled-in land between two piers behind Sutton Place, was a walled and armed fortress. Always, he drew Nita into its protection, when peril threatened.

Her hand tightened on his arm.

"I can't tell yet, dear," he answered her unspoken question. "But he wanted to see me on a matter that could not wait. And an underworld killer tried to prevent him from talking. The fall killed his attacker instantly and, although he was easily identified, it offers no clue. Just a gunnie for hire, but even criminals don't kill without important reasons. This man was plainly desperate, and... Ah, he's coming around!"

THE MAN on the bed opened his eyes, and they quickly focused on Wentworth. "So I made the grade," he said, and grinned—a lop-sided half-deprecating smile that shoved up one quirky eyebrow. "Mr. Wentworth, you've got to go back with me to Schermerhorn. I'm Horatio Smithers on the *Chronicle* there. Reporter. They killed my pal on the paper, like they killed Doctor Holtz."

"Heinrich Holtz," Wentworth interrupted swiftly. "The famous physicist at International Laboratories?"

Smithers nodded. "Doctors said anemia. They're screwy. Can't get the police or even get the *Chronicle* to listen to me.

Listen—" he boosted himself up on an elbow—"Doctor Holtz was murdered for his invention, and when Sam—Sam Dickens, my pal—got hold of it, they murdered him, too!"

Wentworth stared down at Horatio Smithers narrowly. The man obviously believed what he was saying—and someone else believed, too! Otherwise, there would have been no shooting this night.

"They were murdered?" Wentworth said slowly. "Murdered how?"

Smithers reached out a wiry hand, and caught hold of Wentworth's wrist. "Listen, I know what Holtz was working on. Sub-visible and ultra-visible rays—gamma rays. Listen, *Doctor Holtz invented a death-ray!*"

Wentworth jerked his eyes to Dr. Griggs' square-cut face. Griggs was frowning, too. "No, he's not delirious," he said curtly. "Gamma rays can cause anemia—break down red corpuscles. But not quickly. Slow job…."

Smithers said, "Damn it, you've got to believe me! Holtz has found a way to make them work quickly—almost instantaneously. I swear it. Listen…."

He spoke quickly, telling how Holtz and his friend had died, and Wentworth stared down at him intently, feeling Nita's hand still upon his arm, aware of Griggs' taut attention. The only light in the room was a small lamp beside the bed, and its illumination was roseate… So intent were the four of them upon the words that they did not notice the almost imperceptible alteration in the color of the room's illumination.

The one window gave upon the East River which, at this

point, almost washed the walls of the house. It was the source of this change of illumination, scarcely identifiable as any more than a slightly brighter light, as yet. The ceiling was white, and it was there the change first became apparent. Instead of a warm-tinted rose from the lamp, the light there was faintly tinged with green....

Smithers was rushing on, frantically. "A girl I go with was Holtz's secretary," he said. "She told me about this ray. He turned it on rats and, in a few minutes, they were dead. She said the ray was accompanied by a faint greenish light. It could be intensi-fied, in some way she did not know. At its greatest strength, the ray was almost blinding to look at and it seemed composed of both green and orange lights...."

The ceiling of the room was entirely green now. Its ghostly reflection began to touch the faces of the four, to brush the covers of the bed... or was it the reflection?

"Mr. Wentworth!" Smithers pleaded "You've got to believe me! It won't do any harm to investigate, will it? Don't you under-stand, criminals killed Doctor Holtz to get hold of this ray!"

He emphasized his words with jerks on Wentworth's arm. His face was thrust up importunately at Wentworth and, abruptly, his eyes widened. He said, faintly, "Your face looks... *green.*"

For an instant, the words did not penetrate, then Nita uttered a choked scream. At the same moment, Wentworth sprang into action. He whipped Smithers from the bed to the floor, thrust Nita down, and cried a warning at Dr. Griggs.

"Down!" he cried. "Down, you fool! The death-ray!"

The lamp made only a faint rosy splotch in a sea of green

light that seemed, almost tangibly, to fill the room. Wentworth had spotted its source now—the window that opened toward the river. As he stared, the light intensified so that it formed a green shaft slanting upward from the window, filled it from frame to frame.

Dr. Griggs stared at him, frowning, then his jaw thrust out and he strode straight toward the window! Wentworth flung himself across the room in a long, low dive... too late. Griggs stepped full into the beam of the light, his hand reaching futilely upward to draw the shade. His whole body went taut, arched backward. His hands clawed before his face, and the scream that tore from his throat was choked and hoarse with pain. He tottered backward, beating at the air... and then his skin began to smoke. Fumes rose from his face and body as smoke rises from scorching toast, but the stench was the odor of burning human flesh!

## CHAPTER 2
## THE LIGHT STRIKE

WITH A violent effort, Wentworth succeeded in catching Dr. Griggs by the ankle, bringing him crashing to the floor. The screams went on and on, shuddering, horrible, and still the ghostly green light filled the room like tinted air. Even to Wentworth, who had seen so many incredible horrors, this thing did not seem possible. Could light do a thing like this? No, no... He had an almost overpowering impulse to leap to his feet, to challenge that impalpable shaft of light by thrusting a

*RICHARD WENTWORTH*

hand into it—by staring down that funnel of illumination that was no more than so much brilliance scooped out of darkness.

He forced out words. "Lie still!" he called to Nita, to Smithers, and it was equally an order to himself. "Lie still!"

Griggs' screams had dwindled into groans. His body writhed, and Wentworth was forced to fight the convulsive movements of his hands that sought to tear at his face and tortured body.

His face was a crisped mask in which the whites of his eyes glimmered sightlessly.

"Ram Singh!" Wentworth lifted his voice. "Ram Singh, the shutters. Close the shutters!"

His ears had caught the swift beat of the Sikh's feet. They checked, turned back, and presently an electric motor hummed faintly. Across the window, steel shutters slid smoothly. The green light pinched out of the room. With a bound, Wentworth was on his feet, dragging Griggs' body toward the door. Still he did not stand erectly.

"Close to the floor!" he tossed words at the others. "That ray may strike even through steel! Keep away from all windows. Get to the front of the house and call an ambulance for Griggs!"

Ram Singh's big body loomed in the doorway, and a great cry rose from him as he saw the unconscious doctor. Already, Griggs' body was beginning to jerk again.

"Nita!" Wentworth called, as he motioned to Ram Singh to lift the doctor's form. "Morphia for Griggs. Hypodermic!" He swept along the hallway with long bounds, heard Nita cry after him.

"Dick!" she called frantically. "You can't pursue them! That ray would kill you the instant you took off in your plane or speedboat. It's what they want!"

Wentworth knew she spoke the truth, but if his first plan failed, there was no alternative. He could not hesitate. God! Not even an army could thwart criminals equipped with that dreadful ray!

"Take care of Griggs!" he called again. "And call the police— call Commissioner Kirkpatrick! We've got to stop that boat!"

Then he hurried on.

From a wall rack—one of a half dozen scattered over the house—Wentworth snatched a high-powered rifle, lost precious seconds with an ammunition clip. Then he was taking the stairs upward with long leaping strides. He was hat-less, without an overcoat, and, as he flung open the door to the roof, the piercing cold swirled to meet him. A searching, brawling wind plucked at his clothes. It numbed his cheeks, made his eyeballs ache. He sprinted for the battlements toward the river.

No greenish glow edged the rampart or shafted the black sky beyond. He peered through a gun-slit down at the gale-whipped turbulence of the black water. Nothing there; no lights were upon the river. Only distantly, above the low thunder of water against the piles, he could make out the faint mutter of an engine. He could not even be sure of its direction. Wentworth whipped the rifle to his shoulder, pumped two bullets down into the black water, then crouched out of sight. If only he could draw a brief renewal of the attack! But the stormy surface of the river remained blank and empty. The sound of the motor was gone. As furtively as the attack had been made, it was finished.

A SHUDDER, that was not the cold alone, jerked at Wentworth's muscles, as he raced back into the warmth and partial security of his home. He had thought it impregnable to attack! He slammed the rifle back into its rack, snatched coat and hat from a closet and drew Nita with him to the elevator that would shoot him to the first floor of his three-story mansion.

Nita's face was expressionless. A few minutes before, fear had racked her. It still did, but the bravery on which Wentworth had come to depend was hers again.

"Commissioner Kirkpatrick is organizing the police boats," she reported curtly. "Fire boats will help. They'll commandeer any others they can find in commission, but there won't be many at this time of year."

Wentworth nodded. "It's a large boat, otherwise it would not have ridden so steadily, as the light indicated. Diesel motors—I heard them. Phone that to Kirkpatrick."

They stepped out into a hallway, cut through into a small, book-lined room. Wentworth manipulated a lever behind a row of books, and the floor of the entire room dropped swiftly... an elevator.

"Water's too rough for the plane," Wentworth said. "Tell Kirkpatrick to notify his boats that I'll burn two red lights for identification. Tell the ambulance surgeon only what you have to. Warn him to secrecy, and have Kirkpatrick confirm it."

The floor ceased moving and Wentworth moved rapidly through a narrow passageway, came into a boathouse hidden beneath one of the piers that abutted his home. A large and swift cabin cruiser rode there, and Wentworth swiftly threw off the moorings. For an instant, Nita clung to him, then she stepped back. The motors of the boat pulsed into life. The end of the pier lifted soundlessly on powerful mechanism and the cruiser surged out into the turbulent waters of the river....

THE WINTER dawn was graying the east when finally Wentworth drove the cruiser back to its hidden berth and returned with a weariness that was not all physical, into the warmth of his home. The wild night and the utter darkness had conspired to hide the death-boat. The search would be continued, of course, until the whereabouts of every craft on this particular night had been verified. It would be a long and probably fruitless task, for no one had even glimpsed the boat they sought. And meantime? The criminals were at large with their fearful weapon!

As quietly as he had entered, there was one who heard Wentworth and was waiting. Nita van Sloan took his coat silently and brought him a tall glass of hot coffee laced with cognac, then set about preparing food on a small electric grill. She asked no questions, for there was no need. Wentworth's first query was about Dr. Griggs.

Nita's face softened with grief. "He died an hour ago," she said quietly, "without regaining consciousness. Internal hemorrhage, induced by an acute anemia. He was terribly burned."

Wentworth's face was chiseled into bitter lines; his eyes were bleak. He foresaw that Griggs would be but one of many, unless he could find the criminals at once and destroy them. He drained the coffee, rose steadily to his feet—a tall, commanding man with power in the quiet poise of his shoulders, in the taut, flat planes of his face.

"How is that boy, Smithers?" he asked, abruptly.

"He'll be ready to go back to Schermerhorn with you," Nita told him. "I started Ram Singh in the Daimler at two o'clock.

There's a plane at ten, and Ram Singh should be there when we arrive. I've made three reservations on the plane—right?"

Wentworth smiled and clasped her shoulders in his lean, capable hands. "You know how my mind works, don't you, dear? But three reservations?"

Nita's round chin could set with determination, too. "I'm going with you, Dick. You'll need me, and…" Abruptly, she was close to him, her palms hard against his chest. "Dick, I'm *afraid.*"

Wentworth gazed deeply into her violet eyes and knew that it was not for herself that she was afraid. The echo of her panic was in his own breast, too. When and how would the death-ray strike next? God alone knew, but there could be no doubt of the enormity of its menace in criminal hands. No doubt either that the lives of Wentworth and his party were forfeit if his vigilance should fail.

Their departure from his home was furtive as a thief's, and they sped to the airport in a battered car which nevertheless was powerfully motored and bulletproof. Wentworth was gratified to discover only one other passenger, a woman, aboard the plane. There was a foreign distinction to her dress and her modish fur cloak was of exquisite sables. However, Wentworth took the first opportunity to scrutinize her face. When he did, he scarcely restrained a start of dismay!

"No, I can't recognize her by name," he told Nita quietly, "but I've seen her before. No doubt of that I can't even remember where, but in my mind that face is associated somehow with danger!"

ASIDE FROM that one warning, the two-hour flight to

Schermerhorn was uneventful. Horatio Smithers slept fitfully in his seat. Wentworth and Nita strove to put from their minds the horror that lay behind… that certainly lay ahead, also. But Wentworth could not rid himself of his sense of impending peril. Nor could he disassociate it from the modish woman whom he half-recognized. When she also alighted at Schermerhorn, his suspicions crystallized into swift decision.

"You must follow her, Nita," he directed. "Take the Daimler and Ram Singh. There he is, waiting there by the administration building. I'm going directly to the laboratories and, later, to the Holland House. Hurry!"

Smithers' coat was hunched high about his ears, and he shivered as he guided Wentworth toward the taxi rank.

"Don't feel like I'll ever get warm again," he complained. "Sure was a fool stunt I pulled on you."

Wentworth smiled faintly, but his eyes were questing sharply over the field. No one had met the woman Nita followed. So far as he could descry, no one was watching Smithers or himself either. Still, he chose the third taxi in line rather than the one that offered. And he kept watch on their back trail, as the cab skirted Schermerhorn toward the International Laboratories to westward.

Smithers talked in swift spurts about the girl they were going to interview—Margot Mann, who had been secretary and assistant to Dr. Heinrich Holtz, during his experiments with the death-ray. According to Smithers, the nature of his work had been a closely-guarded secret. Under the circumstances, it might be possible to trace out all who had knowledge of the ray and so discover the criminals. It was a slight chance but, at least, it was a beginning. Up to now, there were no clues at all.

"How well do you know Margot Mann?" Wentworth demanded.

Smithers' head jerked about at the abruptness of the question, then his lopsided grin twisted his mouth. "I've known Margot just three years and been nuts about her exactly the same length of time. Hell of it is, Margot thinks she's a career girl. I think I've got her weakening, but—" He frowned at Wentworth's quizzical gaze. "Listen," he said anxiously, "you don't think Margot is mixed up in this thing, do you? Because if you do, you're nuts! That's flat!"

A moment later, Smithers was apologizing for his mode of speech, but he was stubborn in his estimate of Margot, telling what a "swell kid" she was and how Dr. Holtz's death had affected her. Listening to him, Wentworth felt his apprehensions increase. He rapped on the glass, and called to the driver to speed up.

Smithers sat more erectly. "Listen," he began, and swallowed before he could go on. "Listen, you don't think maybe Margot is in any danger?"

Wentworth frowned over his answer. The criminals had found it necessary to kill one newspaperman who had only guessed at their secret. Smithers, himself, had been followed to New York and almost killed to prevent him from telling of his theories. Yet Margot Mann, who presumably knew more than anyone else outside the plot, went unmolested. That indicated clearly either that the girl, herself, was involved—Smithers interrupted violently, as Wentworth argued it—or she was more valuable to the criminals alive than dead.

"The question is," Wentworth concluded, "whether your escape from death and my entrance into the case alters the situation for Margot. Is she still more valuable to them—alive?"

Smithers cried out hoarsely. "God! Why didn't I think of that? I could have warned her…" His voice died away, as he realized the futility of such a warning. "This damned wreck can't do better than forty miles an hour!"

It was another full fifteen minutes before the taxi drew up at the entrance of International Laboratories. Smithers bounded out instantly, and Wentworth barely had time to fling an order to wait at the cab driver, before Smithers disappeared through the swing-doors. He ran after the reporter, saw him take a flight of stairs at an awkward run, his angular body jerking from side to side, coat kiting out behind him.

On the second floor, Smithers continued to run. He twisted his head about to call to Wentworth as he topped the stairs. "Just around the corner now!" he cried. "I'll be damned glad…." His words choked off with a curse. Through the corridors rang the muffled scream of a woman!

*"Margot!"* Smithers shouted. He broke into a frantic sprint, whirled a corner of the corridor and out of Wentworth's sight.

Wentworth's automatic thudded into his palm, and he quickened his own pace to a run. There was a grim hardness to the set of his lips, and he hastily glanced about to locate the possible means of descent from this floor.

He ran on for the corner around which Smithers had

vanished. In the act of turning it, he checked on his toes, flung himself violently backward. The blood drained from his austere cheeks, and the breath whistled from between his clenched teeth. Out from behind the wall of the corridor poured a waxing beam of light—*the green ray of death!*

# CHAPTER 3
# LABORATORY OF DOOM

S CARCELY HAD Wentworth checked beside that corner of death, when the screams burst out. They were all about him, scores of men and women invisible behind closed laboratory doors, shrieking out in fearful terror and pain. And yet there was only this silent, strengthening beam of light, pulsing green in the shadows of the long, high-ceilinged corridor! It was more horrible than if those dying were here before his eyes. The screams rang on and on, all around him only these empty, echoing hallways.

Without analysis, Wentworth knew that few of those victims could be in the grip of this single death-ray that sliced across the hall only inches from where he stood. Many other death-dealing beams must have been loosed. And what of Margot Mann, of Smithers? What of himself? For the moment, he was apparently safe, but, at any moment, another of the rays might slash across the hall and trap him!

He was temporarily safe, only because the killers obviously believed he had been trapped in the first flash of the ray. God, he must find a way... His memory flashed back to the questing glance he had flung about the corridor, on ascending. It was something he should recall. By the heavens—the metal door of a recess in the wall! He had seen it without thought, a few moments before, but now he realized that behind such panels as those, light switches and fuses were usually concealed. Whatever the mode of production of the death-ray, it must depend on electricity. If he could break the circuit....

Wentworth was in motion before the thought fixed in his mind. The metal door was locked. No matter. His automatic crashed twice, battering the lock with heavy lead, warping the metal door. His scrambling fingers found a hold, wrenched. Something like a gasp of relief forced its way from Wentworth's lips, for he was gazing at an elaborate electrical panel! Swiftly, he seized the two main fuses and wrenched them from their sockets. There was a flash of bluish light and, instantly, the shadows of the hall deepened. He whirled—the green ray was gone!

He must act quickly now before the operators could flee, or devise some new means of powering the ray! At full speed, Wentworth raced again for the corner. Despite the fact that the ray was no longer visible, that he knew the power was off, he felt an inner shrinking, as he whirled into the branch corridor. Yet he did not actually hesitate. The echoes of his rasping feet ran with him, for the screams were fainter except that one man was shouting over and over, "Help me! In God's name, help me!"

At the end of the branch corridor was a single ground-glass door. It was through that the death-ray must necessarily have struck. Without checking his pace, Wentworth whipped back his arm and hurled the fuses, he still carried, violently at the glass. A jagged fragment crashed to the floor, and, through the hole in the glass, Wentworth caught a nightmare glimpse of the room beyond.

Across his line of vision darted an incredible figure. It was visible to Wentworth from the waist up, but there was nothing human about it. Arms and shoulders glistened as if made of polished steel and the head—great God, the head was a feature-less metal knob twice the size of a man's skull!

Only for a flashing instant did Wentworth behold the figure, then the hole in the glass went blank. He was still charging forward at top speed. Twice, he squeezed the trigger of his auto-matic, throwing lead high through the door into the ceiling. His only hope—the only hope for Margot Mann and Smith-ers—was for him to complete the panic he had launched among the killers. His mind refused to accept the thing he had seen through the broken glass, but that did not even slow his attack. An instant later, he reached the door and wrenched it open, bounded through. Then he skidded to a halt, with an oath. He was in a laboratory, but no human being, no grotesque mental creature moved. In it was—no one at all!

At each end of the long laboratory, a door stood open, and Wentworth darted toward the one to the right. It was in that direction that the metal monster had moved. On the floor, two men in laboratory gowns writhed and moaned, dying. There was no one else. With an oath, Wentworth dashed back the way he had come, streaked through the corridors and down the steps. In those few moments, while the death-ray burned, the killers had accomplished their purpose—the abduction of Margot and

26

In that ghastly green glare, Wentworth saw one of the policemen stiffen, clawing at the air.

Smithers. What he had thought was panic had been merely the flight of the last of the criminal crew. But if he could overtake them before they left the grounds....

**WENTWORTH'S FEET** skidded on the smooth corridor floors, as he made the last turn and slammed out of the plate-glass doors of the main entrance. He was swearing under his breath, remembering the lumbering slowness of the taxi by which they had come to the laboratories. If it came to a question of pursuit, he was beaten before the start! He plunged to the steps, eyes questing frantically about.

The taxi still waited. Three hundred yards down the main road, a powerful closed car was roaring at constantly mounting speed, already hopelessly out of range. Wentworth was springing toward the taxi, when he caught sight of another machine turning into the laboratory drive, a heavy, powerful limousine. He hesitated only a moment.

"Call the police," Wentworth snapped at the taxi driver. "There's been wholesale murder here. The murderers kidnapped some people and carried them off in that car racing down the road. Hop to it!"

With the words, Wentworth whirled and went with long bounds to meet the limousine, sprang to the running-board.

"Kidnapers!" he shouted, pointing after the fleeing car. "After them, fast!"

The chauffeur stared at him belligerently, but, from the rear, a man's voice rapped out a curt order, and the car leaped forward, lurched into the main road and began to pick up speed.

Wentworth climbed into the front seat beside the driver,

began to fumble fresh bullets into his automatic. He was frowning. Something damnably familiar about that voice from the rear! He twisted around.

The man in the rear was lounging at ease on the cushions, dapper, richly dressed with a sealskin collar on his tightly buttoned overcoat. Above a waxed, supercilious mustache, dark eyes smiled mockingly at Wentworth.

"Wentworth, isn't it?" the man said quietly. "I do seem to meet you under the most extraordinary circumstances."

Wentworth said dryly, "For once, Gerlaine, you're temporarily on the side of law and order. Your arrival was most opportune." He nodded, faced front again to watch the chase.

They did not gain on the fleeing car, but at least no ground was lost. Wentworth's face was impassive, but his mind was racing.

Many things were falling into place now. That woman on the plane! He knew now where last he had seen her—with this man, Gerlaine, in Paris. There was small secret about Gerlaine's activities. He was an international spy, a thief of treaty and military secrets which could be marketed to the highest bidder. No country had ever gained proof against him. The miracle was that more unscrupulous agents had not removed him from the picture long ago by the simple expedient of a bullet in the back. Gerlaine... It needed no puzzling to figure that he was on the trail of the death-ray also!

Wentworth choked back a curse. This time Gerlaine should fail! If the death-ray were ever placed in the hands of unscrupulous war lords, civilization, itself, would be threatened!

Gerlaine's quiet voice, carrying always its suggestion of mockery, came to him from behind. "This really is a kidnapping, Wentworth?" he asked. "If it is... I wonder if it could have any connection with my errand here?"

Wentworth's lips pressed thinly together. "It's a kidnapping all right. If your business isn't with those in the car ahead, you might as well go back to Europe and report failure. Everyone else in the laboratories is dead or dying!"

Fury darkened Wentworth's eyes at Gerlaine's answer. For Gerlaine laughed with satisfaction! "Splendid!" he chuckled. "Then I may take it that the death-ray actually works! Careless of them to let it run amok like that."

Wentworth made no answer, but some communication apparently passed from Gerlaine to the chauffeur, for the car's speed perceptibly increased. He had hoped the death-ray might have been a secret as closely guarded as Smithers seemed to think! Margot's evidence was useless to him now... Yet, if that were so, why had she been kidnapped? Why had all the laboratory workers been slaughtered?

**WHAT PROMPTED** him to whirl about with his automatic at ready, Wentworth did not know, but intuition of peril had more than once saved his life. It did now. His quick turn was just in time. Gerlaine's gun was in his hand and he was crouching forward to strike!

"Just a moment, Gerlaine," Wentworth said quietly. "Better let me have that gun."

Gerlaine assented with a graceful shrug, a smile. "I should have remembered that you are popularly supposed to have eyes

in the back of your head," he
said. "Yes, of course, you shall
have my gun."

Wentworth watched him
hawkishly. The chauffeur
seemed utterly indifferent—
as if, indeed, he knew nothing of what was happening within
a few feet of him. Wentworth, twisted about in his seat, thrust
out his left hand for Gerlaine's gun while his right held his own
automatic ready. It was in the instant that his left hand reached
out for the gun—that the chauffeur acted. He jammed on the
brakes.

It was a perfect maneuver, beautifully executed. Wentworth
should have been hurled bodily against the windshield. It was
a toss-up whether he would be killed or knocked out. But out
of his eye-corners, watching the chauffeur, he had glimpsed the
upward jerk of his knee as he stabbed for the brake pedal. Wentworth had only time to hook his left arm down over the back
of the seat, when the brakes took hold and his own momentum
wrenched him violently forward.

He had a half-view of Gerlaine, one arm braced, lunging to
strike at him with the gun. Impossible for Wentworth to fire at
that instant. Instead, he swiped out abruptly with the barrel of
the automatic, caught the chauffeur a glancing blow on the side
of the head. The man reeled forward over the wheel; his foot
slipped from the brake and the car swerved wildly.

That lurch was more effective than any shot could have been.

Gerlaine was thrown, off-balance, across the tonneau, and Wentworth faced about, seized the wheel of the car—too late.

The heavy limousine skidded into the roadside ditch, jigged up the farther side and hammered its nose in against a telephone post. The post lurched. There was a singing crack, as a brace broke. Its frayed end drove in the back window of the car. Wentworth already had wrenched open the door beside him. The minor jerk of the impact against the post tumbled him, sprawling, to the ground. He was up instantly, lunging toward the tonneau. Gerlaine was slumped, semi-conscious, against the farther side. The chauffeur had pitched side wise on the seat.

Wentworth sprang into furious movement. He dumped the chauffeur to the ground, lashed Gerlaine's wrists with a belt and left him in the rear of the car. A moment later, he was behind the wheel himself, yanking the car violently backward over the ditch and into the road again. The highway stretched ahead, a straight, unbroken line. The kidnapping car had vanished!

Wentworth bore the accelerator to the floor, felt the heavy limousine surge with power. For ten minutes, he burned along the highway at top speed and neither sighted the fleeing car, nor spotted it on side lanes. Anger burned hotly within him. But for Gerlaine's interference, he could at least have trailed the car in which he was certain Margot and Smithers were held prisoners.

Gerlaine's intentions were obvious. He had planned to leave Wentworth unconscious at the roadside and race on, himself, in pursuit. Gerlaine was not concerned with justice, or with preventing the spread of such horror as, this day, had wiped out some of the best scientific brains of the country. He wanted only possession of the secret.

Damn it, he couldn't lose when he was this close to the murdering butchers behind that carnage! He leaned forward and snapped on the radio, spun the dial rapidly to the band of police signals. Silence for a space of minutes, and then the whine of a call sounded, the announcer's voice.

"Calling all cars!" the man said rapidly. "The limousine which left the laboratories just after the murders there had the following license number—JZ-seventy-five-eighty-five. Call back the moment this car is located. That is all."

Gerlaine's voice drawled from the back seat, "Someone, I think, has made a mistake. That is my own license number, Wentworth!"

Wentworth swore softly. Matters were difficult enough without having the police erroneously on his trail. Abruptly, his eyes narrowed in thought. Why had Gerlaine spoken? Since he was a prisoner, it obviously was to his advantage to be stopped by the police. It was true the danger of being stopped was lessening every moment, as the early winter dusk settled… A hidden smile stirred Wentworth's lips and, presently, he parked near a neighborhood drugstore in front of which a delivery motorcycle was standing.

"I'm going to phone the police about their mistake," he told Gerlaine curtly. "And it won't do you any good to try an escape. I've got the key to the car."

HE WALKED toward the store, without a backward glance. But, as he went, he glanced covertly at the license plates, and his smile broadened. Gerlaine had lied about the license number being his own! There were several reasons why he might have done this, but Wentworth thought he knew the right answer. Gerlaine knew where the criminals were hiding and wished to protect them until he could transact his own particular business—or else Gerlaine, himself, was one of the gang!

Inside the store, Wentworth strode directly to the proprietor and started slipping money from his wallet.

"Here's a hundred and fifty dollars," he said rapidly, laying the bills on the counter. "I'm a private detective, and I've got to have your motorcycle for a few hours. We'll agree later on the price."

The druggist, grinning, slid over a key. But before he could answer, the deep hum of the limousine's motor bellowed out, and Wentworth raced toward the door. And he was still smiling. As he had guessed, Gerlaine also had a key to the car.

An instant before he burst from the drugstore, Gerlaine's car spurted from the curb. Wentworth hurled himself at the motorcycle, kicked up its prop and ran with it along the street. It was a half block before the motor coughed and almost a full block before it took hold. Wentworth sprang to the saddle and took the trail of the limousine which already had a lead of nearly a quarter mile. He did not switch on his lights, though the dusk was thick now. No use in alarming Gerlaine. He would think he had left Wentworth stranded.

Before he had gone a half-dozen blocks, Wentworth's thin-gloved hands were numb and cold and his face ached. Astride the motorcycle, he was exposed to the full sweep of the winter wind, and Gerlaine set a hard pace. The speedometer of the motorcycle wavered up to fifty and hovered just above that mark. But Wentworth was content. Gerlaine had made no effort to swing back toward the city. Instead, he was boring through cross-streets, not far from the section in which they had lost the trail of the kidnapers.

It was a half hour later, when Wentworth was winding more slowly among a section of old homes, set far back among trees and overgrown hedges, that he heard the windy whine of a siren racing rapidly nearer through the icy night. On the instant, Gerlaine's car leaped forward at furious speed, whipped around a corner. Wentworth twisted the throttle wide, and the motorcycle sprang ahead. But when he turned the corner, there was no automobile in sight. The siren filled the night now and, in the distance, another was taking up its thin and ominous song.

Frantically, Wentworth wove in and out of the dark streets. He doubled back and quested along the hedges for a break through which the car might have vanished—in vain. As he searched, the red headlights of a police radio car swept into the street, spun a corner. The siren died to a throaty whine, and, a few moments later, the second radio car whipped into sight. An instant after its siren died, a fusillade of gunfire ripped out into the night!

Wentworth swore, wheeled the motorcycle against the hedge, and hurried on foot toward the sound of the shooting. He turned the corner, stopped in his tracks. The two police cars were in the driveway of a huge old Victorian house that sat well back from the road among a forest of shrubs. There was not a light in the building, but the headlights of one of the police cars, sweeping across a rickety porch, showed a man's limp body, half in the front door.

That was all, except that the police were advancing at a sharp run across the lawn, guns jerking in their hands. Then Wentworth's eyes whipped upward to the cupola atop its roof that thrust up darkly against the sky. Was he mad, or had he seen up there a glimmer of… of green light! God, he was right! There it was again!

"Back!" Wentworth shouted and flung himself into a sprint toward the police. "Get back! They're getting ready to kill you from the roof! The cupola on top!"

As he raced, he whipped out his automatic and began to blast lead upward toward that black peak that loomed so ominously against the sky. One of the cops twisted sharply about and began to shoot toward Wentworth. With a violent oath, he flung himself behind a tree while he continued to shout warnings. But how could he make them understand such a thing as a death-ray?

He had been right, terribly right, about Gerlaine. But was he a member of the gang, or merely playing the role of friend so that he might steal their secret? No way of telling. No time to think now of that.

"You fools!" he shouted at the police. "Get back before it's too late!"

ONE OF the police shouted hoarsely. They were lost in shadows now, but darkness would not protect them. The empty windows of the house stared out like blank, glittering eyes. Up there on the roof, there was the glint of glass, too, and then…

and then, the green ray of the death-light stabbed out into the darkness! At first, its broad finger was tenuous, a ghostly hint of a searchlight probing down into the shadows of the lawn. But even as Wentworth stared, frozen with horror, the brilliance of the ray intensified. Like a greedy sword, it cut its swathe through the night—and found its prey!

In that ghastly glare, Wentworth saw one of the policemen stiffen and scream in awful pain—saw his back arch, hands clawing the air. Then the death-ray had swept on, moving gently, silently, a mere glimmer in the dusk—but God how deadly! Another of the policemen was snared in its wide path, pitched writhing to the ground. The ray swept on, making a stately circle about the house.

For moments, the sight again of that awful fight had held Wentworth motionless, and something close to panic stirred in his soul. He flung himself prone on the ground, behind the tree, and began to pump careful bullets up at the light. And nothing happened—nothing except that the screams of the dying rang more loudly, and another man was trapped like a foolish dancing moth in a bath of burning light. A shadow flitted past Wentworth, feet churning the earth and Wentworth caught the glint of terror-strained eyes, saw that the man was a uniformed policeman.

The light was circling again; its range lifted a little. Wentworth sprang up and raced back across the street. Once more he resumed his shooting, with a fresh clip of bullets. Was he mistaken, or was the light dimmer now? Furiously, he emptied his automatic directly up the lane of light. There could be no mistake about it now. The ray was dying. Its brilliance faded, became once more tenuous, was sopped up by darkness and once more the dead stillness of winter night brooded over the scene—quiet save for the moans of the dying.

Furiously, Wentworth flung to his feet. A fresh clip for his automatic and he was sprinting for that black featureless house of death. In a few moments, they might repair the damage to the ray, send its murderous beam reaching out again into the night of prey. If he could reach the house, itself, first… His feet stumbled on the wooden steps, made a tremendous racket across the hollowness of the porch. He sprang past the dead man in the doorway, dived to the floor within, and lay listening.

In all that vast darkness, no one moved, no footstep sounded. Far off, he heard a faint mechanical whirring which he could not place. Cautiously, he got to his feet, sent a narrow beam of light from a pocket-flash questing about. The gaunt hall was empty. Broad stairs led upward. In mid-stride toward them, he halted, listening… There it was again!

Faintly from above, a woman's voice was calling. "Help!" it cried. "Help! Oh, come quickly! The ray! *The green death-ray!*"

## CHAPTER 4
## FIVE SECONDS TO HELL

FOR ONE awful moment after that scream, Wentworth's heart stood still, for he recognized that cry. In his dying moment, he would be able to hear that cry, and answer it. It was Nita who had screamed!

## LEGIONS OF THE ACCURSED LIGHT

The possibility of a trap flashed across Wentworth's mind, but even so he could not hesitate. At top speed, he flung himself at the broad wooden stairs and raced toward the sound of that beloved voice.

"Where?" he cried. "Where are you, Nita?"

Her voice came winging back to him, and he did not need her words to guide him. Up another story, he pounded and through an open doorway from which flickered the fitful light of a candle. For a heartbeat after he flung into the room, he stood frozen in horror.

Three people were bound helplessly against the wall—Nita van Sloan, Horatio Smithers and another girl he knew instantly must be Margot Mann. Their eyes were fixed, in awful fascination, upon a small spotlight set upon a box on the other side of the room. Even as Wentworth's quick eyes took in the scene, a small greenish glow began in that spotlight, focused directly on the helpless three!

With a shout, Wentworth sprang toward the light, whipped it from the box and turned its ray upward. An instant later, green light spilled brilliantly back from the dingy ceiling. Margot Mann sagged in her bonds, and Smithers grinned at him weakly. But Nita's steadfast gaze met his, directly.

"They knew you were coming, Dick," she said swiftly. "I don't know how. They told us, in advance, how long we would have before the green light turned on. I don't understand why they gave us those few seconds of grace."

Wentworth stared at her, drove the daze of horror from his brain. With a quick jerk, he started to disconnect the light cable, but did not. Instead, he focused the green light into a corner and sprang toward Nita and the others. A pocket-knife flipped from his pocket; he began to saw at the bonds.

He was frowning. Ghastly to be working by that green light which had so narrowly brought death, and yet… He flung a backward glance at it. The light was not the same. It could not be. There was a ghostly, all-pervading quality about that other ray which made the very air seem green. This was, purely and simply, a green light. He began to talk rapidly.

"Smithers, why did they kidnap you and Margot," he demanded, "then leave you here?"

Smithers shook his head feebly. "Ask me something easier. They asked Margot some questions she wouldn't or couldn't answer. Same with Doc Canterbury. They kidnapped him from the laboratory with us, but they took him away when they went."

Wentworth frowned with agitation. Nita was free, and he sprang to Smithers while Nita tugged at Margot's bonds. Damn it, there was something wrong here—damnably wrong. Criminals didn't go to the trouble and risk of kidnapping people only to leave them for a delayed death that might be prevented, especially when he was half convinced there was something phony about that green light. They had known he was coming….

"My God!" he whispered. "Get out of this building fast! Nita, take Smithers. I'll carry Margot." He wrenched furiously at the bonds that held the girl to the wall, snapped them loose and swung her into his arms.

Nita was already urging Smithers toward the door. She had learned long ago that it was best to obey when that cold, incisive

40

quality crackled in Wentworth's voice, but Smithers was hanging back, waiting for Margot.

"Damn you, run!" Wentworth snapped. "There's death here for all of us. This house is a death-trap!"

Smithers' mouth gaped. "But you can't know that," he gasped. "How can you know...."

*"Run, damn you!"*

Nita seized Smithers by the arm and heaved him violently out into the hall, thrust him toward the steps. Off balance, he seized the railing and skittered halfway down before he caught himself. With a single backward glance, Nita raced after him. Her face was pale but about her lips was a small smile for Wentworth.

Wentworth went down the steps with great bounds. He could not be wrong. Nita and the others had been left alive for only one reason—to bell him into the building. The light must be a fake, because those who had fled would not risk their dying before he had entered the trap. And now death was anywhere in this darkness. What form the trap would take, he did not know, but there was no doubt it was here.

The stairs, leading down into darkness, seemed seven miles long. The gaunt hallway below, half-illumined by the headlights of the police car, was ghostly.

"Hurry," Wentworth snapped, "or we'll all die!"

STRANGE HOW that light had flickered on, an instant after he entered the room where these three were prisoners. And yet, if it were a fake, the prisoners would have known it a few seconds later. They would not then have called him so urgently into the trap. That was it, certainly. He had been supposed to

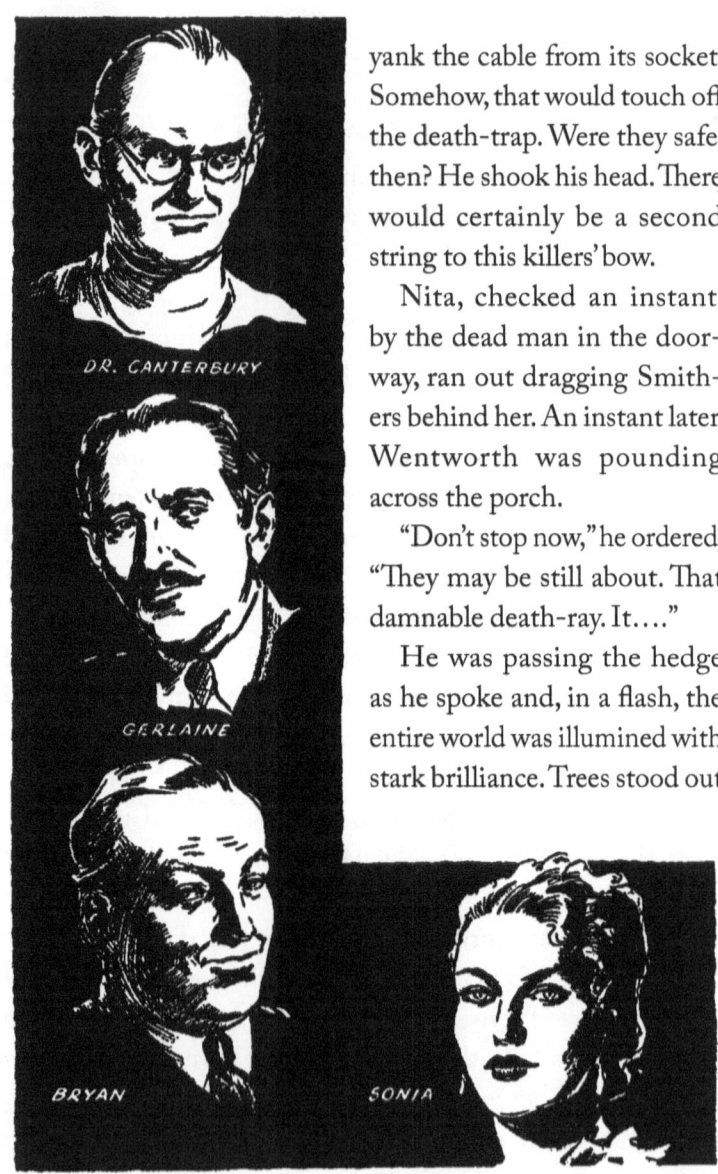

yank the cable from its socket. Somehow, that would touch off the death-trap. Were they safe, then? He shook his head. There would certainly be a second string to this killers' bow.

Nita, checked an instant, by the dead man in the doorway, ran out dragging Smithers behind her. An instant later, Wentworth was pounding across the porch.

"Don't stop now," he ordered. "They may be still about. That damnable death-ray. It...."

He was passing the hedge as he spoke and, in a flash, the entire world was illumined with stark brilliance. Trees stood out as if clipped from glittering metal. A gust of air, then heat, struck him, tumbled him helplessly to the street. He rolled with its violence, felt pressure on his eardrums, a reeling of his senses. When, finally, he could struggle to his feet and stare back, leaping flames had wrapped the house of the death-ray, and were flapping and rolling from every window. Red tongues, like a many-fingered hand, enfolded the cupola high on the roof, roaring like demons.

Dazedly, Wentworth stared about him. Nita was crouched at his side, and he became aware that his arm was about her shoulders and that tremors were racing over them both. Above the roar of the fire, he heard a woman's shuddering moans, but they were not Nita's. Beside him, and a half dozen feet away, Margot and Smithers kneeled.

Wentworth lurched to his feet. "We've got to get away from here," he said thickly. "Back to the laboratory. If they didn't get what they wanted from Margot...."

"But they took this Doctor Canterbury with them," Nita said

quickly. "Dick, I know that dead man in the doorway. He was one of those that helped capture me. I followed that woman to a hotel, sent Ram Singh to call you, and that man—he wore a chauffeur's uniform—walked up to me and said he had a message. While he talked to me, another man took him from behind. The woman registered as Sonia Baklanoff."

Wentworth nodded. He had been a fool to send Nita into such danger, but the information was valuable. It was plain that Sonia was the ally of Gerlaine and he, in turn, was closely associated with the criminals.

"Good," he said, "we'll go for her, first. Smithers...."

"I'm sticking right with you, Mr. Wentworth," the reporter said flatly. "Any man who has hunches like that..." He looked toward the leaping flames, and shuddered. "Mr. Wentworth, I'm your man!"

Wentworth felt queerly drained of strength. His feet dragged, as they walked through the bitter night, seeking a taxi. Yet narrow escapes from death were familiar occurrences in his life. A sudden thought jerked up his head. Three times, he had narrowly missed exposure to the rays of the death-light. Was it possible that weaker emanations had attacked him? When there was time, he would have to have a doctor look him over. He could not afford to be weakened in the midst of battle. But that must come later....

A TAXI, returning from a suburb trip, spun about the corner, and they hailed it—sped toward the downtown district. Wentworth faced the girl, Margot Mann. She was hatless, and the thick coils of her hair made a spot of warm color in the flicker of passing street lights. Her face was firm, the jaw good, the mouth generous. She turned to meet his eyes, and her gaze was open and direct.

Wentworth was accustomed to prompt decisions on character, and he made up his mind instantly that he could trust the girl. Besides, hadn't she been left to die with the rest in that death-trap?

"I think the time has come," he told her quietly, "when you must reveal all you know of Doctor Holtz's invention. Silence now will only assist the criminals. We must know whether there is any protection against the ray, how it is made, and its probable range of effectiveness—whether it will penetrate ordinary substances as X-ray does."

Margot smiled faintly. "Heaven knows, I'd be glad to tell you all I know—but it's pitifully little," she said. "The ray is formed by a combination of gases through which an ordinary electric spark is driven, so that the gases glow. Either a neon-type lamp, or an ordinary Mazda bulb, can be used. I don't know what the gas is, except that it is a combination which took Doctor Holtz four years to achieve."

Wentworth's brows drew together in a frown. This was even worse than he had feared. It meant that the criminals need have no special equipment to produce the ray, other than a bulb equipped with the gas.

"What protection is there against it?" he asked crisply.

Margot shook her head. "I do not know. Doctor Holtz said that even in the lead vault, which is used as protection against the X-ray, he could detect the presence of his green ray—although it was invisible, of course. It was greatly weakened. He was working on that, when I was taken sick during the last week. You see, the last week he was working alone. I think he had found the answer, but I can't tell you anything about it at all."

Smithers uttered a groan. "Better stop talking, Margot," he said. "The more you say, the worse it gets!"

In Wentworth's heart was an echo of the reporter's words. The weapon was stronger than he had feared, and if lead would not stop its rays, what in the name of Heaven would? It was clear now that the criminals knew the secret, that the apparently steel-clad figure he had seen had worn an armor against the ray.

Wentworth felt overpowering despair. He dared not let himself think about the way in which scores of laboratory workers had been wiped out in the International Building. Some of the world's greatest scientists labored there under the direction of its backer, a retired capitalist named Donald Bryan. He had made an early fortune, devoting it, during the last five years, to pure research—or so the story ran. It was a fact, of course, that many of the laboratory discoveries had more than paid for themselves. But it was all wiped out now. God alone knew how many of those famous workers had been killed by the ruthless murderers of the ray—undoubtedly from the desire to make sure that no one else learned the secret of the ray.

The loss was great enough, but it was the utter cold-blooded ferocity of the killers that stirred Wentworth's greatest alarm. If those scores had been killed, the criminals would stop at nothing. Nor could anything stop them! Police—even armies—would be powerless before the onslaught of the ray.

"The world must not know," Wentworth said thickly.

Smithers whipped toward him. "Are you crazy? The world's *got* to know! They've got to be warned."

Wentworth smiled thinly. "And just how would you arm yourself against the ray?" He leaned forward, hammered sharply on the glass. "Stop at the first telephone booth."

Already, he saw the course he must follow. Washington must censor the news! Smithers was staring at him glassily. He started to speak, then his mouth closed, and a stubborn look crept into his face. Wentworth could read his mind as clearly as if he spoke aloud. It would be the same thoughts that would ride newspapermen throughout the country. Suppress a big story like that? Nuts! So it must be Washington....

The taxi slewed to the curb. Wentworth went swiftly into a drugstore and called Washington. Only one man would suffice. He must reach, the President, himself! But first he called the Department of Justice and spoke to a high executive there, arranged to get through to the President. Wentworth's name and voice were known there, but three quarters of an hour elapsed before the deep, emphatic voice the nation knew so well reached his ears.

Wentworth plunged immediately into a description of the things that had happened, of what he personally knew of the death-ray.

"I can't expect you to take my word for this, sir, I realize," he said finally, "or to take such a drastic step as censoring the news on my say-so alone. But you can recognize the danger inherent in the situation. These criminals must be fought and exterminated. If police and the people know in advance what faces them they will flee in panic from every glimpse of a green light. Ignorance means many deaths, but knowledge means a panic throughout the nation that may destroy our very civilization! You'll have to declare a national emergency, sir, secretly, and prevail upon the news services! At least, stop these stories for tonight, and rush your own investigators to the scene."

The President's voice was grave. "I'll investigate at once," he replied quietly, "and if your findings are confirmed... I promise that what can be done will be done at once!"

WENTWORTH LEFT the booth with a lift of his heart. Such promptness and efficiency in high places was the greatest safeguard the American people could have. Yet, it was a drastic measure Wentworth had urged. He believed it necessary, but he might fail. He must *not* fail! He must track down the criminals and destroy them, before *they* destroyed the nation he loved!

As he hurried back to the taxi, Nita's voice winged out to meet him. "Dick! Dick! The radio...."

Wentworth sprang to the cab and caught the lifting excitement of an announcer's voice.

"The death that wiped out three-quarters of the personnel of International Laboratories this afternoon," the man said rapidly, "has struck again within a few hours! From Ashville comes the report of curious green lights which played over the walls of the county jail there. Our correspondents tell us that every official and inmate of the prison is believed to have been killed! No explanation can be found for the attack. There was no attempt at a delivery, and this recurrence of the mysterious deaths...."

Nita snapped off the radio and her eyes, meeting Wentworth's, were wide, frightened. "I remember now! In that awful house, one of the men said something about... about having a little practice before they tried Conestoga. Ashville is *a little practice....*"

"Conestoga?" Wentworth echoed the word almost vacantly. That prison was where the incorrigible criminals of the state were lodged—the most vicious killers who still evaded the chair, the masters of the rackets. Wentworth beat a clenched white fist on the door. He whispered, *"Conestoga!"*

His eyes burned into Nita's and their gray-blue irises turned cold and bitter. The intention of the terrorists was damnably clear. Not content with their frightful weapon, they were bent upon building an invincible army—recruiting their legions from the prisons! At Conestoga, they would release ruthless hordes and launch upon America its most diabolical wave of lawlessness—a saturnalia of rapine and murder. In his wildest imaginings, Wentworth had not pictured such a hell on earth as this! He whipped inside the cab, slammed the door.

"Step on the gas!" he ordered, and there was a metallic edge to his tone. "The Holland House, as fast as you can drive." He sat rigidly, his face grim. His course lay clear before him, though he knew that defense of Conestoga prison, facing the fierce stabbing death of the ray, was foredoomed.

"Nita, you'll return to New York," he instructed. "Report full details to Commissioner Kirkpatrick. I'd like Miss Mann to go with you to give Kirkpatrick's experts the benefit of such knowledge as she has about the ray. Smithers, you call the governor, personally, and report what we know about Conestoga. Cite what happened at Ashville. I'll back up your report, at the first possible moment."

Nita's hand rested tensely on Wentworth's arm. "And you, Dick?"

Wentworth's lips curved in a stiff and ominous smile. "I," he said softly, "am flying to Conestoga!"

## CHAPTER 5
## THE SPIDER FIGHTS

AT THE Holland House, Wentworth delayed only for brief moments, but, when he sped toward the airport, Nita and Margot Mann beside him, he carried death with him in a suitcase—his own death, if its contents should be discovered by officers of the law. Within that suitcase were the habiliments of the Spider!

Nita knew that dread secret, as did the valiant Ram Singh—but there were few others. Wentworth had need to guard the fact well. Though the Spider fought always for justice, his methods were not those of the law. It was precisely because the safeguards, which must be maintained for the innocent, were perverted into a shield for vice, that the Spider had been born. His swift and unswerving justice had struck where the law could not reach. He had been a thief in the night, a merciless executioner—but always for the ends of justice.

Yet the law could take no account of his motives. In its eyes, he must remain a murderer—and so his mere identification as the Spider would mean his doom! Nevertheless, Wentworth did not hesitate. It would be the Spider who fought at Conestoga—the Spider whose name and reputation for swift vengeance carried terror to the underworld. If any man alive could stem the criminal tide that would flood at Conestoga, it was the Spider. No, he would not hesitate.

Nita said nothing to dissuade him from the course she knew he had chosen. But she sat very close to him, as the powerful Daimler, Ram Singh at the wheel, pushed its sleek nose into the rising wind toward the airport. She longed to go with him into battle.

"It's a wild night for flying, Dick," she said quietly. "Are you sure there's nothing further to do here?"

Wentworth's lips were grim. "I've lost the skirmish in Schermerhorn," he said, "and the criminals have left the city. Eventually, the battle may shift to New York. That is inevitable when this Terror has gained enough strength. Commissioner Kirkpatrick must be ready. Meantime, I want him to frame up some charge against Gerlaine and get out a nation-wide general alarm for him. I still can't believe that he's the one behind all this, but he seems to have close contact with the criminals." He looked beyond Nita to Margot Mann.

Nita had given Margot a hat, and the cloak's fur collar was high about her throat. She was a lovely thing with the fresh color of the cold in her cheeks, but there was no smile on her full lips.

"Margot," Wentworth said, "can you get Nita a picture of Doctor Canterbury?"

The girl's head jerked about toward him, and she drew in her breath sharply. "Oh, you think he's guilty? I've been thinking about him, but I scarcely dared speak. He's a great scientist, and yet it seemed to me he was... *snooping* about Doctor Holtz's laboratory a lot."

"You and he are the only laboratory workers left alive," Wentworth pointed out with a shrug. "The Terror and his men carried off Canterbury, though he told them, *in your presence*, Margot, that he knew no more about the invention than you!"

Ram Singh wheeled the Daimler to a halt close against the administration building marquee at the airport. Dry fragments of snow were spitting down the wind, whisking against the windows with a soft hissing. A wild night. Wentworth bowed his head into the cold thrust of the breeding storm and hurried Nita and Margot to shelter. The warmth of the waiting-room gushed out to meet them, and Wentworth strode directly toward the manager's private office. As he neared, the door swung open and Wentworth barely controlled a violent start. A woman was leaving the office. Her dark eyes lifted boldly to Wentworth's and about her full lips played a slight, mocking smile. Wentworth masked his surprise, clicking his heels in a precise bow, recognizing the woman of the plane—Gerlaine's assistant, Sonia Baklanoff!

"Madame," he said formally, "I should have recognized you on the plane. I had, in fact, but it was not until I met your... compatriot, Mr. Gerlaine, that I could be sure."

Sonia Baklanoff's sensuous lips bared her white teeth, but in anger. "That dog!" she cried. "Do not mention 'is name to me!" WENTWORTH MURMURED his apologies while he suppressed a smile. Did Gerlaine think to fool him with any such schoolboy pretense of dissent? While he made introductions among the women, Wentworth's eyes went beyond Sonia to her escort. The man was big, florid. With crowfoot wrinkles about his shrewd eyes and jovial small mouth, he presented an innocuous, if care-worn, appearance.

"M'sieur Donald Bryan," Sonia introduced him, "who had such unspeakable misfortune as to lose his staff of coworkers in the International Laboratories! Ah, those ruthless, so cruel American criminal!"

Wentworth's attention flew to Bryan, the organizer and head of the laboratories. He did, indeed, seem haggard. It came to Wentworth fleetingly that, of all men, Bryan should have been most conversant with Holtz's work since, as laboratory director, he would receive reports.

Bryan spoke heavily, his voice full and deep. "I'm afraid you're in for a disappointment, if you want a ship, Mr. Wentworth," he said. "All regular trips have been canceled because of the weather. I can't persuade the manager to charter a plane, although it's imperative for me to reach Washington promptly."

Wentworth masked his swift concern. "Are conditions as bad as that?" he demanded sharply of the airport official.

"Sleet," the man replied succinctly. "Ceiling three hundred feet, and lowering. Hurricane winds at five thousand feet."

In the moment of silence that followed, the voice of the wind rose to a wild shriek.

Wentworth frowned. "Can't blame your pilots, under the circumstances." He shrugged, bowed to Bryan and Sonia. "It looks as if Washington and New York would have to wait for us." He strolled back to the exit, drawing Nita and Margot with him.

But, once outside, his demeanor changed.

"Back to the city for you and Margot." Wentworth had to bend close to make himself heard above the shouting wind. "Catch a train for New York. Tell Smithers to keep an eye on Sonia and Bryan."

"But *you*, Dick!" Nita cried.

They faced each other, buffeted by the storm, faces stung by the hurtling icy snow. In the dim light from within the building, Nita's face showed pale and worried.

"I'm flying to Conestoga," Wentworth said doggedly. "The Terror and his men have a start of hours. A night like this is ideal for their purposes."

Nita moved close, peering up into his eyes. "Dick, you must let me go, too. Then, if anything happens…."

"Nothing will happen," Wentworth replied crisply, "and Kirkpatrick must be warned. After Bryan has left, I'll be able, at least, to buy a plane and pilot it myself. Go now, darling."

For a moment longer, Nita clung to him, then she turned crisply toward the Daimler. Nothing in the erect carriage of her shoulders betrayed her alarm. Wentworth watched the tail-lights of the car quickly blotted out in the thickening storm and, a few seconds later, Bryan followed with Sonia. That combination troubled him deeply, but at the moment he could not spare either the time or thought for them.

He must act now.

WITHIN TWENTY minutes, he had made his deal with the airport manager and a small but powerful cabin job was wheeled out to the runway. Six men clung to its wings to secure it against the wind. Wentworth wasted no time on talk. He climbed into the ship.

An instant later, motor roaring wide open, his plane was snatched aloft by the storm. As quickly, it lunged downward, and, when he managed to lift the nose, the ground-lights of the field showed dangerously close through the murk.

Moments later, he was flying in a storm-dark world in which sky and earth alike were invisible. The ship twisted and shuddered, bucked like a living thing. If it held together, Wentworth thought grimly, he would probably break a world's record on this flight. The wind was on his tail. He managed, finally, to pick up the radio-beam to Albany.

In an incredibly brief time, Albany swept past beneath him, identifiable only by its radio signals. Wentworth began to angle his way across the wind. It was impossible to estimate his side-drift, and despite sickening swoops, he gradually reduced his altitude until he could occasionally glimpse the rolling barren hills or ice-bound fields. As nearly as he could estimate, he was already in the vicinity of Conestoga prison, but he could recognize no features of the landscape. Ice began to form on the wings so that he was forced to rocket upward again.

Nevertheless, Wentworth was certain he was somewhere near

his goal. He began to work over the countryside in a vast circle, skimming downwind at prodigious speed, buffeting against the gale on the swing-back so that the plane plunged and bucked. When, finally, a cluster of lights showed briefly below, Wentworth put the nose of the ship down. It had been a momentary glimpse through a flaw in the storm and almost at once the lights were gone. When again he spotted the town, the earth was perilously close. He forced himself to be gentle with the stick, and leveled off not a hundred feet above the roofs. An unusually tall steeple, an up-thrusting hill in his path would mean almost certain annihilation, but he fought to maintain his low altitude.

Delicately, he jockeyed the nose of the plane into the wind. Each gust threatened now to dash him to earth, and he manipulated controls with lightning-like reflexes—gradually cut the throttle until the ship seemed to hover almost motionless in the eye of the wind. Slowly then, he drove north and west to seek a landing-place. He did not know the town below him and was trusting, as much to his flying instincts as to instruments, when he decided that he must be somewhere in the general vicinity of the prison. From here, he would make the trip in an automobile—if he could land.

It seemed an eternity that he battled so against the elements. Ice was forming on the wings with alarming rapidity. He must act at once before the ice changed his wing conformation, robbed them of lift and dropped him helpless to the earth. The scattered lights of the town were thinning out. A few tree-broken fields began to show. Grimly, Wentworth made his choice.

Against this wind, he would have to go down with his motor roaring—and trust to luck and skill.

He yanked the red knob that released a landing-flare. It was instantly whipped away by the wind, but he caught a glimpse of the icy earth and eased the stick forward. Swiftly, the frost-hardened field rushed to meet him. Another flare showed briefly that it was cut by ditches, studded with fieldstone, and his run would be cut short by a ruined wall just high enough to rip the undercarriage off the plane. But his choice was made. He slammed the tail skid hard down against the ground.

Instantly, as the motor slowed, the wind swooped on the ship, savagely. It shied sideways. Wentworth cut the ignition, and deliberately dug his right wingtip into the earth in a ground loop. He had a flashing glimpse of the dark earth, pin-wheeling across his vision. There was a ripping crash....

AFTERWARD, THE coldness of the storm reached in through the rents in the cabin's wall, and Wentworth realized that, though he hung dizzily upside down in his straps, he was unharmed. Clambering free, he saw that his ship had looped into the gnarled branches of an ancient apple-tree and seemed soundly anchored. Aside from the smashed wing-tip, a bent propeller and the holes branches had punched in the fabric, it was not badly damaged.

Wentworth was not concerned with it. He dug out his suitcase from the ship, and turned toward the village. Then he made out the swing and bob of a lantern carried by a man afoot. Now, if he was not too far from Conestoga...?

His flying instincts, he found, had guided him well. He was at

Stony Brook, a bare twenty miles from the prison. Within a half hour, he had bought an ancient car and was plowing through the stormy night. The exhaustion of the flight left him quickly, and he began to frame plans.

He was not sure that the attack on Conestoga prison would be made tonight Yet, as he had pointed out, conditions were ideal—and Wentworth was confident the Terror would waste no time in organizing his criminal machine. First of all, of course, Wentworth must get in touch with Albany and discover if proper precautions were being taken. Yet, what preparations could be made against a death from which there was *no* protection?

It was midnight when Wentworth drove his steaming, heavy car into the deserted streets of the town of Conestoga, and began his hunt for a telephone. He found one in an all-night restaurant and was suddenly aware of a consuming hunger. He ordered food, went into the phone booth. It was minutes before the operator answered, and then it was only to report that the storm had crippled the service. There had been no communication with Albany since shortly after six o'clock!

Wentworth's lips tightened at that news. It meant the warden at Conestoga had not been warned! Probably they would know nothing, either, about the carnage at the laboratory and the Ashville jail unless some official had happened to listen in on the radio. Would they heed Wentworth's warning? Damn it, he would make them!

Rapidly, Wentworth went over the means at his disposal. His name would mean little to the warden, without endorsement from Albany—if indeed his identity would be believed. On the other hand, the warden doubtless would feel constrained to act upon an anonymous phone call. It would be worse than futile to warn him specifically against the death-ray. Mention of such a thing would cause the warden to doubt his entire story.

Wentworth decided to eat before making his call since, in this sleeping town, it would be simple for the warden to trace the message. He kept his face muffled between pulled-down hat-brim and overcoat collar, while he ate rapidly of the heavy food. Then, once more, he entered the booth and called Conestoga prison. After seeming hours, a man answered harshly.

Wentworth disguised his voice. "I gotta speak to de warden, right away," he said hoarsely. "Listen, it's a tip-off on a crushout, see?"

The voice at the other end of the wire quickened, and presently another man was speaking.

Wentworth raced out words. "There's a crushout planned, maybe tonight," he said rapidly. "A mob is going to start trouble outside. De signal is a green searchlight. The minute any mug turns a green light on de prison, you better start shooting wid evert'ing you got. Remember what happened at Ashville!"

Wentworth hung up on the warden's sharp queries. If he knew by the radio what had happened at Ashville, he was warned against the ray. Otherwise, nothing Wentworth could say would help. He hurried out of the lunchroom, got the heavy car rolling and started on a roundabout course for Conestoga. The warden would send guards and police to find him, and he had no intention of being a prisoner during that battle he was certain lay ahead.

The storm seemed to increase in intensity. Wind rattled and drummed about the ancient car. Snow crowded thickly against the windshield so that the wiper labored, and the headlights lost strength thirty feet from the lamps. Wentworth had his hands full to keep the car to the road, at twenty-five miles an hour.

HE FIGURED it was almost precisely an hour after his phone call that he brought the heavy car to a halt. It was in a narrow lane to the lee of thick woods near the prison, and he peered through the slanting gray streaks of snow toward the lights of Conestoga. Searchlights were alive atop its walls, their restless fingers prodding thick darkness, inquiringly.

Wentworth nodded in satisfaction. His warning had been heeded. Climbing into the back of his car, he set up and opened his suitcase. A trap with a mirror and strong, battery-fed lamp, provided him with a makeup table. He set swiftly to work, after covering the windows.

A liquid coating tautened and swallowed the skin of his face so that it stretched shinily over the cheekbones. The lines of his mouth were altered so that it became a lipless gash. The nose, rebuilt with putty, became hawk-like, predatory. It was all, save for bushy black brows to cover his own and a lank, long wig, but the face that stared back, cold-eyed, at him from the mirror, was the face of the Spider! With quick gestures, he drew a trailing black cape across his shoulders, tugged a slouch hat low on his brows. His hands traveled briefly to twin automatics nestled beneath his arms.

The Spider was ready for battle—against hopeless odds! Many times had he fought against what seemed certain death but never when such a weapon as the death-ray was arraigned against him!

Wentworth thrust aside worry over the peril he could not avoid. Thoughtfully, he removed the suitcase from the car and hid it amongst some shrubbery. It was while he crouched over the hiding-place that he heard the deep throb of a powerful automobile engine above the creak and moan of the storm among the barren trees.

Bending far forward, he scuttled along the lane until he was hidden within five yards of the highway. Headlights were boring through the storm, and, presently, Wentworth made out the lumbering form of a wrecker towing another machine. When he could make out the details, he saw that the disabled machine was a prison van with solid metal sides and barred windows!

A puzzled frown knotted Wentworth's forehead. The van came from the direction of the town and might have carried guards there to search for him. Perhaps, it had broken down or had an accident. Nevertheless, his suspicions were aroused. He pulled out an automatic and ran swiftly along the roadside. But, now, a searchlight within the prison had picked up the wrecked van and was holding it as it trundled toward the gates. Still Wentworth could make out no challenge, no signs of excitement. Apparently, it was expected for, a few moments after it came to a halt before the iron gates, those portals swung open.

While Wentworth hesitated, the wrecker truck lurched forward with its tow. Halfway through, it appeared to stall, jamming the gates wide open. At the same instant, Wentworth caught in the distance the wide-open roar of racing engines, speeding down the highway.

Wentworth shouted, sprang to his feet—too late. For aboard the wrecker, stalled in the gates, the batteries of work-lights flicked on and began to play over the stone walls atop which the guards paced. Where those lights touched, a ghastly green-ish glow sprang up... *and men screamed horribly!* As quickly as that, it happened!

# CHAPTER 6
## THE BATTLE OF CONESTOGA

WITH A violent oath, Wentworth flung himself into the battle. He was too far from the prison gates for effective shooting, and he desperately sprinted nearer. He could see more clearly now. Four batteries, of three lights each, were affixed to the wrecker, and these apparently rotated mechanically, since they were methodically sweeping the walls though no one visibly, controlled them. Four wall searchlights were focused on the wrecker, and heavy gunfire racketed down the wind; the deep discharge of riot-guns and the rattle of rapid-fire weapons.

Through it all, the green death-rays swung placidly, steadily, about their work with a mechanical persistence that was horrible. Where they touched, guns fell silent and men screamed....

Wentworth saw all these things while he raced, feet skating and sliding over the ice, to get within range. Finally, he flung himself prone and began a deliberate fire on the ray-lights themselves. Three times, he threw his lead at one of the death-ray lamps, and three times the vibrations of the lamp told him he had scored—but the light still blazed on! Even its steady sweep, like the inexorable swing of an executioner's sword, was unchecked. Not until he had emptied an automatic did he realize the truth—the lights were shielded by bullet-proof glass, impervious to his attack!

He half sprang to his feet to rush closer. Then, abruptly, he remembered the drum of other motors which he had heard at the beginning of this assault. Even as the thought flashed into his mind, he spotted the machines racing toward the prison with dimmed lights. Three more wreckers, each bearing clusters of the death-dealing lamps! Once more, Wentworth flung himself prone and, whipping out his second automatic, opened fire on the trucks. He sent one searching bullet toward the driver's side of the windshield, hopefully. But, with a tightening of his lips, he realized that only the more difficult target of a tire could avail. The windshield, too, was bulletproof!

With only the illumination of the dim headlights, he was shooting more by instinct than actual vision. Twice more he fired without result, then the first truck lurched wildly, swerved toward the ditch where Wentworth crouched!

With a frantic leap, Wentworth sprang aside, as the front wheels of the heavy wreck thundered into the shallow ravine. A gun blasted at him redly through the darkness. Wentworth twisted, pitched to earth, and fired at the flash. A man cried out hoarsely and, an instant later, the batteries of death-rays thrust their murderous beams at the walls. God, he was so helpless!

He had warned the prison, even arrived here in advance—yet there was so little he could do!

Already, while he dueled with his first wrecker, a second had raced past the gate and was sweeping the walls beyond with rays. The third machine had lurched from the road and around a corner of the wall. Presently, from its direction, too, came that awful green glow of death. Already, the gunfire of the guards had virtually ceased. Even the screams of the dying had faded. In a few moments, men would dash inside to free the convicts. A ravening horde of human beasts would be released upon the countryside and, with the wires down, no warning could go out! It was up to the Spider, single-handed....

IN THE gates of the prison now, Wentworth could see men whose garments seemed molded of polished steel and whose heads were encased in huge spherical helmets. Two were beside the batteries of lights in the farther truck and, as he spotted them, the batteries ceased to revolve as units—and a single ghostly green finger probed toward where he lay!

The death-ray swung overhead so closely his uplifted hand could have touched it. Once more, Wentworth knew a feeling of utter incredulity. Even as he burrowed more closely against the frozen earth, he found himself doubting the reality of the things that were happening. That beam above him was a lovely, though sinister, thing. The ray seemed a thing of substance, a smoky, moving mist, in which the slanting snow vanished—that stained earth and air with its sickish deathly glow.

The beam moved on, questing, and, by its reflected illumination, Wentworth saw other moving figures in the near-by wrecker—saw that those batteries, too were being separated while the death-rays quested over the walls to seek their individual prey!

If he made the slightest move toward the wrecker, or fired a single shot, those rays would swoop toward him like pouncing eagles! Must he then lie here, helpless, while the Terror fulfilled his purpose and recruited the legions which would strip the nation? A curse that was half-sob squeezed out between his locked teeth. There was a way! There *had* to be a way! By the heavens—*the car in the lane!*

Cautiously, Wentworth rose to his feet and, bent double, raced back toward the woods lane. Once a green ray raced toward him, and Wentworth pitched prone into a shallow ditch. His body crushed through thin ice, and the frigid water ate like knives into his flesh. But he lay motionless, and the seeking light swept on.

Immediately, he was on his feet again, running, and, seconds later, beside the car. Rapidly, he tore the curtains from the windows, the mats from the floors and soaked them with gasoline from the tank. He heaped them in the tonneau and, without lights, sent the heavy machine trundling toward the highway. If he should be spotted and those death-rays turned upon him?

Already, a few convicts were beginning to trickle out through the gates. There were over two thousand in Conestoga. Surely, the Terror did not intend to enlist them all in his army of death! How would he transport them? To what use would he put so many? No matter. His intention was plain, and they must be turned back within those walls, or else—or else, they must die!

Wentworth's car jounced into the highway, straightened out

toward the prison, and Wentworth drew out a book of matches from his pocket. Already, the car was gaining speed. At any moment, the sound of the motor might reach the men of the Terror, and draw their lethal rays. No, he could not wait.

Wentworth struck a match, touched off the whole book and tossed it into the gasoline-soaked rear. At the same moment, he

On the watch tower of those prison walls, the Eye of Flame traveled like the finger of death!

yanked wide the hand throttle and hurled himself to the road-side ditch. An instant later, the green rays, like sentient feelers, picked up and held the car. But it was past stopping now, by any such means as that. With flames and black smoke boiling from its windows, the roar of its engine deepening, the car careened down the road toward two of the wreckers!

Jarred and shaken by his fall, Wentworth lay through a half-dozen long breaths in the ditch. Narrowly, he watched to see if his leap had been spotted, but apparently all the death rays of the two trucks were concentrated on the car. Now was his chance—now while attention was focused exclusively on the car.

With a leaping rush, Wentworth crossed the highway and crouched no more than fifty feet from the rear of the wrecker whose tire he had blasted. At any moment, he might be spotted and he knew how instantaneously those rays could kill. He must work fast. Already, the blazing Juggernaut he had freed had passed the first wrecker, and was speeding on while the death-rays still sought it out. A low-sweeping beam brushed the prison gate, and two escaped convicts fell screaming in their tracks!

A shout of triumph leaped to Wentworth's lips, but he choked it back. His Juggernaut was holding true to its course. It would ram the second wrecker squarely in the rear. Now the men there were realizing that the rays would not avert the charge of doom. Two of those in polished armor leaped to the ground. Another apparently tried to get the wrecker away. The engine started and it trundled a few feet forward out of Wentworth's line of vision. But the Juggernaut had gained too much speed. Triumph swelled in Wentworth's soul. By the heavens, he had found a way!

HE WAS within fifteen feet of the first wrecker, and the two men were staring the other way. Just as the Juggernaut crashed, blazing, into their comrades' machine, Wentworth flung forward in a sprint. The Spider's cape flapping out behind him, like the wings of some bird of death, he hurdled bodily into the wrecker!

With the full force of his leap, he drove his shoulder into the back of the nearest armored man. The man's helmeted head snapped back as limply as a rag doll's. His arms flung wide, and he catapulted out into space. Before he struck the ground, Wentworth seized the second man, shoulder and crotch, lifted him high above his head and flung him bodily after the first! Wild laughter pumped from Wentworth's chest.

He sprang to the controls of the death-rays! One he whirled so that its misty beam spilled across the two unconscious men and once more Wentworth laughed—the mocking, menacing laughter of the Spider. For the helmets of the two men were gone and, under the rays of their own lights, they writhed and died!

Scarcely pausing to observe the results of the attack, Wentworth whirled an entire battery of lights and brought them to bear directly on the open gates of Conestoga! Men were rushing those gates from within, and the green light mowed them down like a prodigious blade. Wentworth cupped his mouth with his hands.

"Back!" he cried. "Back to your cells, or you die. *The Spider commands you!*"

Screams broke loose within the prison walls, and Wentworth glanced swiftly about him. The second wrecker and his car were a tangled and flaming mass of wreckage. The death-rays there were extinguished. But the two men, who had leaped free, faced toward him. Guns blasted in their hands!

Wentworth's automatic kicked pleasantly against his palm. One of the men faltered, then came on again! Wentworth cursed and crouched low behind the bullet-proof cabin of the wrecker. Was that armor to spoil his maneuver?

Rapidly, he fumbled with the back of the cabin and found the low door that opened there. An instant later, he flung behind the wrecker's wheel and kicked the motor to life.

So long as no death-rays were turned on him, he was safe in this bullet-proofed cabin. Also, the two men, who knew of his presence and his attack, were before him. Wentworth's lips curved stiffly. He stepped on the gas and let the clutch come in with a jerk. For a split-second, the tires whirled on the ice, then they bit through to gravel, and the wrecker lunged forward in a head-long charge!

Muffled screams came from beneath the helmets of the two armored men. They tried frantically to leap aside, but their armor was heavy. One stumbled, and fell prone. The other slipped to hands and knees in his effort to climb out of the ditch. Then the wrecker clanged against their metal sides. The men were down. Wentworth wrenched the wrecker out of the ditch and swiftly, his eyes went over the scene. Guns were cracking at him from the prison yard, but no living person showed in the gaping prison gates. For the first time since the beginning of the battle,

Wentworth began to hope for victory. There was only one other wrecker left, aside from the one that was jammed in the prison gates, helplessly. Apparently, its crew was busy freeing convicts. The fourth wrecker was around a bend.

WENTWORTH GROUND down on the accelerator. Because of the flat tire, his machine was hard to handle. It tugged violently against the steering-wheel. It took all his strength and ingenuity to hold it on a straight course. The greater his speed, the more difficult his task. Yet, he must hurry. Once let the killers in the other car learn what has happened, and he stood no chance at all.

Wentworth's lips set grimly as he battled the wrecker toward the bend around which he knew the other machine of the Terror was at work. Even as he raced to the attack, he spotted the headlights of the wrecker stabbing around the corner of the wall. It was a hundred feet away and, he guessed, coming to the attack! When it swung into sight, he must send his own truck crashing into it.

Desperately, Wentworth fought to get more speed out of his captured truck. It yawed wildly. The flat tire whined and banged beneath the front wheel, threatened momentarily to throw the car into the ditch or caroming into the wall. The hood of the enemy truck was thrusting into one side now, fifty feet away. In another instant, they would be able to bring their death-rays into play. Fifty feet, but the truck would not hold a true course even ten feet after he took his hands from the steering-wheel!

Wentworth jammed the accelerator to the floor. The entire truck was clear of the wall. Two men in armor were at the controls of the death-rays, sweeping the walls above. They were holding with both hands against the heavy lurching of their car over the frozen ground. As Wentworth watched, one of them jerked at his companion and pointed toward the charging doom now rushing upon them. Wentworth thought he could hear a muffled shout. One of them grabbed the controls of a death-ray, began to swing it around.

Wentworth's breath caught in his throat. Which would strike first? Would the death-ray strike him before he could slam into the wrecker? But it was obvious that it would. A wrench of the wrist would bring that green killer slashing through the bullet-proof glass. If the truck would hold true for only twenty, for fifteen feet... By the heavens, he'd make it! He wrenched open the door beside him, ready to jump. At the same instant, the tireless wheel whanged against a boulder.

For a mad instant, Wentworth fought, one-handed, against the wrench of the wheel. It tore from his grasp. The truck yawed about in a tight semi-circle, reared on two wheels and flopped violently over on its side. Wentworth felt himself propelled through space. He had a whirling glimpse of green death-rays, fire and prison walls. There was just time to double himself in a tumbler's ball, when the ground came up to meet him.

HE STRUCK on his shoulders, rolled violently and felt the sharp stab of broken underbrush... then he was lying still and gazing up blankly at the lowering sky. The stinging bite of snow particles prickled across his face. Had he been knocked out? Wentworth wasn't sure.

He lifted his head cautiously, began testing arms and legs. His whole body ached, but there seemed to be no broken bones. He pushed himself to his knees and stared toward the prison. Before it blazed two fires, and he saw that the second wrecker had either ignited when it crashed or been deliberately set ablaze. As he watched, scores of men in convict garb scurried out through the gates. Others were already stripping the armor from the men he had killed.

He had failed—terribly. The hordes were released upon the helpless, unwarned people!

For a mad moment, Wentworth wavered on the verge of opening fire on this loosed army of crime, but well he knew the futility of such an attempt, single-handed. Not even the Spider could stem this tide now, unless....

On hands and knees, in the middle of that frozen field, Wentworth studied the serried ranks of convicts, mustered and commanded by the men in armor. Abruptly, Wentworth knew what he must do. Cautiously, he rose to his feet and crept close to where men prowled about the fringes of the mob. Presently, he spotted one who slipped off alone into the darkness. Wentworth trailed him silently, was on him with a rush. His heavy gun swung once, then swiftly he stripped off the convict's clothing and donned it—racing off toward the spot where he had left his suitcase. But half of his job was done.

Behind a screen of shrubs and trees, Wentworth once more set to work with his make-up tray. The wig vanished and pomade grayed his hair. A few moments sufficed to change the Spider's lipless gash into a pendulous mouth. Then Wentworth drew from a compartment a pair of hooded spectacles which he donned. He hid the suitcase again and shuffled off to drift gradually into the fringes of the convict mob.

He was a man now whom many of them would recognize, a small-time crook who had a pretty skill in safe-cracking—one Blinky McQuade whom a premature flash, in a safe-blowing, had almost blinded. Such was the underworld identity Wentworth had built up in New York's slums to assist in his ceaseless battle against crime.

If the convicts remembered that they had not heard of his presence in the prison, what difference did that make? Easy to say he had just arrived—had been sent up for cracking a crib in Schermerhorn. Yes, he was one of the convicts and to morrow he would be one of the Terror's men—until he learned the Terror's secrets and identity. And then....

Meantime, Wentworth stopped beside the body of one of those he had slain, and pressed to his forehead the base of a slim, platinum cigarette-lighter. When he straightened again, there shimmered on the white dead flesh a vermillion seal that shone curiously in the flickering light of the fire.

"Hey," a convict near him whispered, "find anything on him?"

"You said it!" Wentworth whispered back, his voice quavering. "Look at his face. See that spot? It's... the seal of the Spider. *The Spider is on our trail!* Know what that means, eh?"

## CHAPTER 7
## THE DEATH MARCH

A S THE man shivered and slunk away, a new plan of battle was taking shape in Wentworth's mind. He did not know the intentions of the Terror, concerning the escaped convicts. But plainly they would move in a body for a while, and there were few of the Terror's leaders here. If he could isolate and remove them one at a time—leave the dead beneath the seal of the Spider—he might drive the convicts into a panic that would make them easy victims for the posses which soon would start after them.

Yes, that much the Spider could accomplish. But he would be no nearer, afterward, to the Terror and the knowledge of the death-ray and armor which he must have if he were ultimately to annihilate the killers. His first move must be to learn their plans....

Wentworth pivoted, at a long, piping blast on a bugle which rang out shrilly on the cold air. Then he swore softly and, as all others were doing, moved toward the wrecker which stood before the prison gates. A man in armor stood on the roof of the cabin, stood in a full glare like the limelight of a theater—but the spotlight he used was a concentration of all the death-rays upon the truck! He stood in an aura of that awful green and lifted his arms. The murmur, that had started among the convicts, was stilled.

Wentworth crowded closer and peered up at the glittering figure which seemed a very incarnation of the death-rays. He started violently, for this man's helmet was not blank as were the others. Instead, upon its face had been executed a single enormous eye that extended entirely across the front of the helmet! Was it possible that this man was—the Terror himself?

Wentworth's hand slid toward his automatic, until he remembered that the armor was bulletproof. He began to swear under his breath. Once more, the figure lifted its hands and a deep voice, muffled yet resonant, began to roll out words.

"I am the one who has freed you," he said sonorously, "so that you can join my army. Before I turned you loose tonight, I destroyed all the wires that might give the alarm. It will be hours before anyone tells of the escape. By that time, we will be miles away."

He paused, and a rising shout of applause rang out over the massed hundreds of criminals.

"I am going to break open every prison in the country!" the Terror cried. "We will be so powerful that no one can stop us. We can strip whole cities of their wealth—and no one can raise a hand. If we were not strong enough to do this with ordinary weapons... *the Eye of Flame shall do it for us!*"

As he spoke, he swung his arm in an abrupt powerful gesture and one of the lights swung from its focus on his armor and strayed to the prison wall. A man stood there, bound to one of the watch-towers—a gray-haired man Wentworth recognized as the warden! The green light now rested fully upon him!

As his screams rang out, a muffled roar rose from the convicts. The warden writhed and fought terribly against his bonds, as the dark fumes of his burning flesh began to rise.

Wentworth ripped out his automatic and fired once from the hip, directly at the doomed man—saw him collapsed into merciful death. He had acted without premeditation, intent only on saving that brave man pain. But, instantly, he saw that he might have destroyed all his plans. He cursed himself for a fool, thrust the gun away. He stared about him with a dazed face, as other men were doing.

"Who did that?" he demanded angrily. He seized the shoulder of a man beside him. "Did you do that?"

A cry of fury swelled up from the convicts at being cheated of their prey. Anger roared, too, from beneath the helmet of the Terror.

"Bring me the man who did that!" he commanded.

Wentworth's lips drew tight. What a fool thing to place all his plans in jeopardy to save one man a few minutes of torture, even though that man were very worthy to be saved. He would have to work fast. The thing was done. He swung an arm high.

"Here he is!" he shouted. "I saw him shoot!"

He shook the shoulder of the man he first had challenged, ran his hand inside the man's coat and pulled out—Wentworth's own gun! "Here's the gun he did it with!"

INSTANTLY, THE convicts closed in upon the man, ignoring his shouted frenzy. Wentworth allowed them to take him away from his grip, and was, himself, shoved into the rear. The victim was a man he recognized, a racketeer who had made his tens of thousands in narcotics and doomed thousands to the living hell of dope addiction. Wentworth had no scruples in making him the scapegoat....

Moments later, the man was thrust up to the hood of the wrecker, where the Terror still stood. The racketeer shrieked aloud that, he was innocent, but the Terror's voice bore him down, reached out to the farthest limits of the crowd.

"I am the *Eye of Flame!*" he boomed. "It is best that you learn now not to go against my wishes and commands!"

The great glittering helmet bowed toward the still protesting man, and Wentworth, gazing at the huge eye which decorated its front, saw that the pupil and iris of that eye had become a *glowing green.*

Even as he saw these things, the glow brightened and, from the eye, a narrow beam of light—misty, hideously beautiful—reached out and rested upon the racketeer! He screamed for fifteen minutes before he died beneath the torturing narrow beam from the Terror's enormous eye. All around Wentworth men shivered with a coldness that had nothing to do with the wind and the storm. And when the man was dead, no single whisper of a voice could be heard.

Slowly then, the beam of the death-ray faded, and withdrew, and the Terror spoke.

"Thus do I punish those who cross my will!" he thundered. "Remember it! Also, that I reward those who serve me well. Now, we march! Within an hour, we will reach the railroad. On the sidings, there are two freight trains. Enter those and, by daylight, we will be in Catskills. Men, that town is yours! The Eye of Flame will help you loot it!"

A mutter, then a cheer, swept up from the liberated convicts. Many of them swung about and moved off toward the railroad, with the Terror's voice booming after them.

"Reward for those who obey. For those who fail me—*the death!*" As he finished, the death-rays died. He stepped down from the cabin of the wrecker, and it began to trundle along the road.

Wentworth marched with the convicts in a daze of rage and apprehension. He knew the Terror spoke the truth when he said the wires were down. With daylight, these savage hordes would descend on the unsuspecting city and destroy it—unless the Spider gave warning!

Wentworth's bitter gaze swung to the wrecker which, with the Terror aboard, led his army of destruction. Worshipful convicts ran close beside it, keeping up a constant cheering. No chance to strike at this leader; no time to spread the fear of the Spider and so scatter this mob.

Somehow, he must travel ahead of it to Catskills. But he must contrive, also, to remain one of the servitors of the Terror, for in no other way could he finally best this incredible warfare. Wentworth's thoughts were cut short by a hand clapping him violently on the shoulder, a muffled voice booming in his ear. He spun to confront one of the men in armor.

"For cripes' sake, Blinky!" the voice came out. "When did you get sent up?"

Wentworth scowled—as Blinky McQuade, that scowl was invariably above his weakened eyes. "What's it to you?" he snarled at the figure in glistening armor. "And who in hell are you, anyway, hiding out in that tin monkey suit?"

The man chuckled. "Still the same old Blinky," he said. "I'm Monk Burton. You come along with me. The Eye is looking for some safe-crackers to do some special jobs in Catskills, and you're supposed to be pretty good."

Hope sprang up in Wentworth's heart. Perhaps, now he would get his chance to strike at the Eye. Once that were accomplished, the mob of convicts would disintegrate. It needed some special fear and dominant strength to bind them together, and with that removed....

He glanced sidewise at the big-shouldered man in armor. Monk Burton was a strong-arm man, once a minor big-shot in New York's rackets, but his participation in the work of the Terror told Wentworth nothing. Wentworth clumped along behind Burton, but he did not see the Terror. Instead, he was shoved into a freight car with a score of convicts, some of whom he recognized as pete-men. Behind Wentworth, a man in armor who might, or might not, be Burton—he could not tell—climbed into the car and locked the door. A few minutes afterward, the train lurched into motion.

"All aboard for Catskills!" one of the convicts sang out, and the others laughed raucously.

Wentworth saw that they had been provided with a few bottles of whisky which already had gone the rounds. He was in a rage with himself. He had been a fool to let Burton bring him to this moving prison from which he would be unable to escape until Catskills was reached. Yet he had had no alternative. If he had refused, Burton's suspicions might have been aroused. WENTWORTH STUDIED the armored guard. It might be possible to overpower him, but, if he did, the convicts would be certain either to kill him or turn him over to the Eye. Even if he escaped the train, what could he hope to accomplish with the wires all down? It might take him hours to find an automobile. Hopelessly, Wentworth realized that his only chance was to remain with the train and, on arrival in Catskills, make his escape and flash a warning to the townspeople.

On the faint chance that someone might find a message, and be able to get a warning through, Wentworth dropped a series of notes from the train, at deserted stations past which they clanked, at road crossings in the country—

All the convicts have escaped from Conestoga. They are going to loot Catskills, hundreds of them. Warn Catskills to watch all freight trains for convicts.

The Spider

It was six o'clock, the still cold darkness before dawn of a winter morning, when the train finally groaned to a halt in Catskills and the doors of the box car were thrown open.

"Quiet!" the man in armor warned.

Wentworth went to the door with the rest. The storm had ceased, but a cold wind stirred faintly now and again and sent the dry snow rustling in little swirls and gusts of white. It was bitterly cold, and the convicts cursed and shrank back to the protection of the car. Wentworth fumbled his way to the ground. The man in armor stood in the doorway.

"Stay close!" he warned sharply.

Wentworth grumbled, but made no direct answer. If only he could tell when the man's eyes were on him! But there was nothing to indicate. The steel knob of a helmet never turned. It was, apparently, fastened solidly to the cuirass, allowing the head free movement within. Damn it, he had to escape without arousing suspicion. He sidled back to the door, rested a hand on the floor.

"Hey, give a fellow a hand!" he snarled up at the man in armor.

The man bent and held out a hand. What happened then was too quick for any eye to follow. Wentworth yanked savagely on the outstretched hand, at the same time thrusting against the man's ankles. There was a muffled cry and the man arched out into space, turned a half-somersault and landed violently upon his back. Wentworth was beside him in a moment. His fingers found the fastenings of the helmet and released it, while the man lay half-stunned. Instantly, Wentworth's hand slid through the opening, and his stiffened fingers jabbed sharply into certain nerve centers in the throat.

Men stood in the doorway of the car now, calling down questions in a subdued tone of voice.

"Geez," Wentworth said harshly, "how do I know what happened? The lummox slipped and took a nose-dive, I guess. Can you walk, buddy?" He bent over the unconscious man and, altering his voice, made a hoarse answer.

Afterward, he dragged the man to his feet, drew an arm across his own shoulders and took a hold about the waist. In the half-dark, it would seem, to the watchers in the car, that he walked. Wentworth twisted his head about, "He says for you to stay in that car or he'll bang your heads off when he comes back."

Then he walked heavily off into the darkness with his burden. It strained Wentworth's strength to the utmost to manage the big man with his weight of armor. As soon as possible, he checked in the shadow of a pile of ties and rapidly began to remove the ice-cold armor from the man's body. He bound and gagged his prisoner, thrust him into the ravine and bridged ties above him, jammed into the banks, so that he was completely hidden.

**IT WAS** an awkward task, in the darkness, to climb into the pieces of unfamiliar armor. His mind was racing with plans. How long it would be before the Terror organized and launched his attack, he had no way of telling. He would have to move swiftly. The armor gave him one immense advantage. He could move anywhere among the convicts without challenge—and he was safe both from the rays and bullets.

Fifteen minutes after he had yanked the guard from the doorway, he was striding off through the pitch darkness of the dawn. He could see plainly in all directions through the helmet, though he could not guess how this was achieved. Nor was there time now to speculate. His metal-clad feet skidded wildly on the snow, and the touch of the armor pierced coldly through his clothes, as he hastened along beside the train.

Queries were shouted down at him. He answered them all that he was "going for orders," and did not pause.

It seemed an eternity that he tramped along the tracks before he spotted the lights of the town off to the left. He looked carefully around to see that he was not watched, then ran heavily for the shadows of a freight depot. He reached it without challenge, hurried on. He had driven through Catskills once, and now searched his memory to recall the design of the streets. He knew that it was a manufacturing city of some seventy-five thousand persons. Surely, in such a place, he would be able soon to find an accessible telephone to reach the police.

With a sickening sense of futility, he realized that in a city of this size there would be, at most, five hundred police—probably not many more than half that number. It would take a half to three quarters of an hour to assemble even so many as lived close to headquarters. If only he had been able to get a warning to the city earlier, it might have assembled the National Guard troops.

A block beyond the depot, he turned into a broad street which he recognized. It would swing up into the main part of the city. On a corner stood a shabby lunch wagon, its windows opaque with steam. The slippery steel on his feet was maddening. Twice, he fell before he reached the diner. He clumped up the steps without delay, slid the door wide, with a crash.

Behind the counter, a somnolent worker lifted his head. He stared wildly and tremors began to shake his body. There were two men slouched over the counter. They twisted about. One of them uttered a shrill scream and, dashing the glass from a window, began to clamber out. The other whipped out a revolver and opened fire!

Wentworth felt the double punch of two bullets against his breast plate and faltered for a moment in his stride, then went on. With a shriek, the gunman fled as had the other customer before him. The man behind the counter still stood, motionless; a small, strangled sound forced its way out of his throat, his eyes walled up and he slumped to the floor.

Behind his helmet, Wentworth frowned bitterly. If his lone appearance frightened these men so, what must be the result when the cohorts of the Terror marched up the streets—when the green death-rays lashed out and the convicts rushed to plunder!

He spotted a wall telephone, realized he could not reach his pockets and, irritably, punched the cash-register button for a coin. It took five minutes to make the police sergeant on duty answer his phone. Lord, how could he make these men understand what lay ahead? How to make them believe his incredible news? He spoke crisply into the telephone, altering his voice, with sudden inspiration, to an official rasp.

"Sergeant?" he said curtly. "Sergeant whom? O'Hearn. Very well, Sergeant O'Hearn, this is Brown, adjutant general of the state. The wires have been down—I couldn't reach you sooner. All the convicts have escaped from Conestoga prison. Yes, *all!* Listen to me, Sergeant. There is no time for foolishness." Wouldn't the fool ever shut up?

"The convicts seized two freight trains and, by this time, are probably very near Catskills—if not already there. Call out all your reserves. Summon the national guard, also. Waste no time. The men are heavily armed and desperate. Open fire on sighting them, and shoot to kill. You understand, Sergeant O'Hearn— *shoot to kill!* Throw a strong guard about all your banks. Have the men erect barricades across the streets and take positions on house-tops. I shall hold you responsible, Sergeant O'Hearn!"

The man stammered unintelligible sounds into Wentworth's ears and he fought for restraint. God, what hope was there that the reserves would be summoned in time? What chance of defending the city?

"Don't stutter at me, Sergeant," Wentworth interrupted coldly. "Start calling your reserves. Who is the commander of the National Guard in Catskills? Who? Very well, I'll call him, myself. For God's sake, Sergeant, move swiftly. I have just had a fresh report that the convicts have actually reached Catskills!"

Wentworth slammed up the receiver, and a bitter smile twisted his lips. The "report" he had heard was the far-off, faint wailing of a bugle. The Terror was summoning his cohorts to battle!

## CHAPTER 8
## LOOT! LOOT! LOOT!

IT WAS easy to put over his deception on the half-awake local commander of the national guard and, once the warning had been given, the man was prompt in his response.

"I'll put men into action as swiftly as possible, sir," he said curtly. "I'll have to summon them by telephone, but I have an arrangement I worked out with the telephone company here, during the last strike, which should turn them out fairly fast. I think I can promise you some prompt action, sir!"

Wentworth snapped, "Congratulations! God help your city, if it has to depend on the police for protection! Don't lose an instant."

He slammed up the receiver and hurried from the store. Far off, he heard the wail of a police siren, and swore under his breath. Either that fool sergeant was rushing his only available men to the railway to be killed, or one of those who had fled from him had phoned the police—even before his own call had gone in. He sprang into a dark areaway behind the diner and his lips tightened into a harsh line. A police emergency wagon swept past carrying a dozen men.

Wentworth sprang out and shouted. But the only response was the deep roar of a riot-gun that splattered pellets across the chest of his armor. The car skidded violently around a corner and, moments later, he could hear it jouncing over the rutted railway tracks. Furiously, he flung himself forward. As suddenly, he checked, and felt despair eat into his heart. For, from the corner where the car had sped, a green light was glowing.

Wentworth did not have to hear the screams of the dying, nor the rending crash of the wreck, to know that a dozen brave men had been wiped out without firing a shot in the defense of the city. For once, the Spider stood irresolute. His plan called now for his return to join the cohorts of the Terror, to cement his position there so that, when this day's horror was over, he would be one of those who went to the Terror's headquarters. Only in that way could he ultimately defeat the madman killer who called himself the *Eye of Flame*.

But could he leave this city to the destroying hordes? He, alone of all who might come to the city's defense, knew anything about that deadly green ray which could wipe out scores of men with a single lick of light. He, alone, might tell them how to combat it, as he had fought it before Conestoga prison. There was just a chance that he could make the defenders listen to him.

Wentworth's bowed head lifted. Actually, there could be no hesitation. He must do what he could for this doomed city and, afterward, find a way to resume his place among the Terror's men!

With the decision, Wentworth whirled back toward the lunch wagon. It was deserted now, and he strode directly to the phone, once more called the commander of the national guard, Colonel Rogers. He caught the man on the point of rushing to the armory.

"Colonel Rogers," Wentworth said heavily, "there is more to this than a mere escape of convicts, I have learned. The prison was smashed open from outside. I know that sounds incredible but it happened. The men who did this have a new and powerful weapon—a death-ray. Damn it, Colonel, do you think I called up at this time to make jokes? I said a *death-ray!* I know of no protection against it, but the machines which produce it will be mounted upon trucks.

"You can smash these trucks only by charging them with other trucks. I warn you than any man, struck by the light from this ray dies instantly. Your only hope is to let the trucks run wild—to blockade streets so that the enemy machines can't get past. You will use your own judgment as to tell your men about the ray. Steel may retard its action for a brief while. The enemy—some of them—have an armor which turns the ray and also is proof against pistol bullets. I imagine your rifle bullets will pierce it. That's all, Colonel. God be with you!"

AS WENTWORTH slammed up the receiver, he could hear the shouting roar of the convicts and knew that the march upon the city actually had begun. He left the diner, hurriedly. To his left, dotted by street lights, stretched the main thoroughfare of

Catskills. It climbed a slight rise toward where the dawn showed gray and silvery against the eastern sky. Down its middle ran a single set of tracks—from the police truck that had gone with all its men to its doom. Spotless snow for the murdering feet of the army of death!

From that main street, the town slanted away on the south toward the railway tracks, but, on the north, climbed toward the residential heights of the city.

Instantly, surveying that prospect Wentworth knew what the plan of defense must be. If heavy trucks were gathered atop the hill and sent roaring, at full speed, down the side streets—if others were poised there where the silhouette of Main Street lifted against the dawn sky, to charge into the hellish death-ray machines of the Terror—there might be a chance. But there was so little time! The convicts were on the march and Colonel Rogers had just left for the armory. Others might be expected to arrive within a few minutes afterward, and only then could organization of the defense of Catskills begin!

Wentworth plunged to the sidewalk, fought his way with back-sliding feet up the first of the cross streets that slanted up toward the residential section. He would do what he could to delay the convicts and permit Colonel Rogers to organize. More than that, he could not do. If he showed himself to the guardsmen in his present garb, he would be shot on sight. He would fare no better if he stripped off the armor, for, under it, was his stolen convict's garb. There was no time to find any other. The mob-roar of the convicts had reached Main Street!

Peering fearfully behind him, Wentworth saw a broad shaft

of greenish light spring into being, thrusting its deadly beam up Main Street. Above the tops of the low-squatting tenements near the railway, the green glow built up. Good God, it was massacre! The Terror was killing right and left along his line of march, without regard for whether the people he slaughtered attempted to oppose him! Already, the tortured, horrible screams of the dying rose upon the chill thinness of the dawn air!

Frantically, Wentworth ran on. In the shadows beneath skeleton trees now, he could make out three automobiles parked at the curb. They would not have the shocking power of trucks, but he must use what he had.

Swiftly, he raced to the first, smashed his mailed fist through the window beside the driver's seat and wrenched open the door. It was the work of an instant to release the brakes, throw out the clutch. But he had to put his shoulder to its back before it began to roll through the night's fall of snow. Finally, he had it moving and could spring to the running-board to guide it. At the end of the block, the car was doing twenty miles an hour, but its momentum was mounting—and it had held its course well.

Wentworth sprang from the running-board, lost his footing in the snow, and fell heavily. Instantly, he was up and racing back toward the other two cars. Once, he twisted his head about and saw the car he had released, sidling off toward the right-hand side of the street. It was a question whether it would crash before it reached the corner. The shouting was very near.

Wentworth raced back up the hill, turned once more as once more he neared a parked car. The runaway scraped the right-hand curb, swerved back. Its movement seemed pitifully slow and inadequate. It lunged back and leaped the curb just as three men in armor turned the corner by the diner.

Wentworth heard their muffled shouts and then the car slammed into them, skidded sideways and slued out of sight around the corner. Frightened shouts rang gratefully in Wentworth's ears, as he released the brake on the second car and started it after the first. Of the men who had fallen, only one of them was moving. He struggled up to hands and knees and crawled out of sight around the corner.

A fleeting question arose in Wentworth's mind as to whether he had been spotted, an apparent traitor in the garb of the men of the Terror, but he thrust it from his thoughts. He was committed now.

He sent the second car rolling on its way, dropped off before it got fairly under way, and hurried back to the third. He had it rolling before the second car had reached the first intersection, and this time he clung to the running-board—sprang to the ground and thrust his shoulder against its side to hurry its pace.

If he could send the two cars crashing together into the leading truck of the Terror! A score of feet beyond the intersection, Wentworth could no longer keep pace with the car. He flung himself aside, ran lumberingly for the cross-street above.

With a groan, he saw the first car he had started begin to swerve toward the right-hand curbing. Its front wheels jammed in the snow, flung it into a broad side skid. It turned completely around, trundled backward a half-dozen yards and rammed futilely into a tree. But the other was going strong and, even as Wentworth watched, the first of the Terror's trucks rolled into sight. A sound between a curse and a prayer forced itself out between Wentworth's close-pressed lips.

The men on the truck had sighted it now. They were shouting to the driver. The truck surged forward, but its tires spun on the smooth pavement. It slued sideways and, in the same moment, the runaway car rammed home against its hood. Locked together, the two machines skittered completely across the street.

Wentworth choked back a shout of triumph, and darted for the corner, raced uphill parallel to Main Street. He could not tell how much damage had been done by the collision, but, if he had managed to cripple the steering-wheel of the truck, or smash a wheel, it would be enough to put it out of the battle for the present.

ON THE next street, only one car was parked, but it was a heavy sedan of ancient vintage. He wheeled it to the middle of the street, stood the cushion on edge to jam the steering-wheel in place. Even as he paused, calculating the best time to release it, a truck thundered past the base of the street and was gone.

With a curse of disappointment, Wentworth released the car. Instead of slowing the attack, he had speeded it! At least, he had prevented the slaughter of some of those who lived along that line of march, for, at this speed, he doubted that the rays would have time to penetrate effectively through brick walls.

As he released the car and hurried desperately to reach another street, from which he might launch a similar attack, Wentworth heard shouts behind him. From a side street, a half-dozen convicts, led by one of the men in armor, debouched. One carried a sub-machine gun, which he lifted. Slugs kicked up little flurries of snow, churning their way toward Wentworth.

One of the slugs struck his leg and knocked it out from under him. Pain lanced up to his thigh from the blow. But now Wentworth's own automatic, which he had worn strapped outside his armor, was in his hand. Prone on the ground, he answered the fire of the attacking party.

There was a thin twist to Wentworth's lips, beneath the helmet, and he shot with the deliberation of a veteran upon a target range. His first bullet drilled the machine-gunner dead-center, spilled him limply upon the snow. The man in armor bent over heavily to retrieve the weapon, and Wentworth concentrated on the other members of the party.

His next two shots dropped two more convicts and, with screams of terror, the others turned and ran. But the man in armor had the machine gun now. Probably, he wasn't too expert with the gun or one of the convicts would have carried it. Yet, even in a blunderer's hands, the weapon could be terrible. It fired the same cartridges as Wentworth's own automatic, but its longer barrel gave it greater impact. If a concentration of those slugs should hit in one place!

Wentworth ignored the man, as he lifted the gun, and concentrated on the weapon. He knew it with the intimacy of an expert and exactly where to place his bullets. The man in armor fired two bursts, before Wentworth could spot his lead. His second shot yanked the machine gun from the man's hands and spun it, disabled, into the snow.

An instant later, Wentworth was on his feet, charging. It

seemed a mad thing he did, and the nerve of his enemy was shaken. He retreated two stumbling steps, turned to run—then Wentworth crashed into him with his shoulder. Wentworth spilled to his knees. The impact sent the armored man a full ten feet through the air. He struck on his head—and the helmet *shattered!*

Wentworth stared in amazement at the glittering shards of the helmet that flew upward, glistening, into the air. The man lay where he had fallen. Wentworth ran to him, caught up one of the fragments. They resembled a heavy glass, with a reflective coating upon one side, and there were the usual laminations of bullet-proof glass, layers of cellulose material between.

It was an accident, then—this thing that had happened. The man wore a defective helmet. Wentworth's lips quirked at memory of the fact that his own helmet might be faulty, too, and that he had, nevertheless, confidently braved the fire of a machine gun. He shrugged, but he had gained knowledge. A rifle bullet would drill those helmets!

Abruptly, the air about him was filled with the green misty glow of a death-ray! It swept past him, lingered briefly upon the houses on each side of the street, and was gone. But, where it had touched, heart-rending screams broke out!

That ray was incomparably more powerful than any he had seen in operation before. At less than a second's exposure, it had penetrated house walls to kill the innocents within! Even behind stone walls or shields of steel, men would not be safe from those deadly emanations—not even for the space of time necessary to discharge a rifle!

AS IF in echo of his thoughts, Wentworth heard a brisk volley of rifle-fire break forth—to die as instantly as if a titanic sound-proof door had been closed! Dimly, men's screams drifted down a chill morning wind that was like the breath of death.

Wentworth peered down toward Main Street. The last car he had released had rolled futilely through a swiftly cleared lane among the marching convicts. It was wrecked against the stores on the opposite side, and only a single crumpled body lay upon the snow to mark its passage. And the last of the ray machines had passed. The battle of the Juggernauts was finished. From now on the Spider would fight from among the ranks of the Terror.

Grimly, Wentworth reloaded his automatic, as he strode downgrade toward the streaming cohorts of convicts. Easy enough to rejoin the army. They would think him the man who had been sent to stop the Juggernauts—and, since they had ceased, he now wore the crown of success. He had given the guardsmen as much time as possible. God grant that they had been able to organize along the lines he had urged, for there was no other way. Perhaps, he might help them capture a ray-machine and turn it on the convicts. Perhaps....

Wentworth strode out into Main Street and stopped, stood rigidly while his eyes swept upward along the line of march. He could not strangle down the groan that rose to his lips. For the battle of Catskills was over, and the victory was to the army of crime!

Up there, where the crest of the hill marked the city's center, the rim of the sun—red as if it rose through the flowing blood of the city's defenders—made macabre silhouettes. The crest of the hill was held by a swarming throng of convicts, and two of the ray-machines. Their death-lights were faint against the waxing sun, but they were triumphant. For not a single gunshot answered them.

## CHAPTER 9
## THE TERROR'S TRIUMPH

THROUGH LONG moments, Wentworth stood motionless. About him, convicts were shouting hoarsely in triumph. He saw them smash the windows of shops, heard the cries of the looters. And there was no one to oppose them, for the rays had swept clean.

A cold and killing rage swelled in Wentworth's breast. It took all his Titan's will power to reason coolly that his one gun could do little to avenge the horror perpetrated here—unless he could strike down the Terror, himself, and destroy his headquarters where rays and armor were stored. He forced himself to stride through the marauding hordes toward the crest of the hill where the ray-trucks were concentrated. The snow that had been pure white and trackless was now a filthy, muddy smear.

Wentworth recognized that his armor was dangerous. Undoubtedly, the few who wore it were known to the Terror and, while its anonymity would protect him from discovery during battle, it would make his detection as an impostor only the more certain once the looting of Catskills was consummated. On the other hand, it was clear that the Terror must plan to abandon most of his convict allies. If he took any with him, it would be the experts he could use in future raids. He might take Blinky McQuade, who had an amazing skill with safes!

At the thought, Wentworth looked more attentively about him. A gang of convicts was smashing the windows, tearing at the iron screens that guarded a jewelry store. At intervals, along the street, men in armor stood like sentries. Instantly, Wentworth's plan was formed. He hurried into a dark hallway and quickly stripped off the armor. Then, putting Blinky McQuade's spectacles on, he hurried toward the nearest of the armored men.

"Look," he said gruffly, "maybe you don't know me, but they's plenty as does. I'm Blinky McQuade, and what I can't do to a safe you'd bet can't be done."

The blank helmet confronted him, but the man inside said nothing.

Wentworth prodded the metal chest, "Why in the hell don't you make a noise, or am I talking to a dummy?"

The man grunted, "Keep your paws off, punk."

Wentworth twisted McQuade's mouth into a fawning grin. "Okay, okay, I just wanted to know. They's a bunch of guys scrapping over a jewelry dump down the street. Youse go wit' me, and I'll crack de safe, an' split fifty-fifty wit' the Eye, see? I ain't goin' to open dat crib for dem mugs. How's about it?"

The helmet continued to stand dumb. Wentworth peered up at it through McQuade's hooded glasses, shuffled restlessly. "Okay, okay," he grumbled. "Skip it. To hell wit' it. I'll go up and talk to de Eye. Maybe he won't t'ink you're so smart."

He started off, and a steel-covered hand reached out and

gripped his arm. "You'll open the safe," the man's voice came out muffled. "We'll take the swag to the Eye, and you'll take what he gives you. The Eye will play square."

WENTWORTH COULD scarcely keep the grin of triumph off his lips. That was exactly what he had hoped for, but he did not assent too quickly lest the armored man grow suspicious. Finally, he agreed and, with his armored guard clumping beside him, shuffled toward the jewelry shop.

Knowledge of safes was part of the rigorous training of the Spider. The strong box in the jewelry shop was at least five years old and depended more upon electric alarms than on impregnability. It took him twenty minutes of work, after the guard had cleared the shop, to fathom the safe's combination. Jewelry and uncut stones, which Wentworth estimated roughly at two hundred thousand dollars, were dumped into cardboard boxes. Then, with the armored man, Wentworth started up the hill.

He grumbled, because it was Blinky McQuade's habit to grumble, at submitting to the partition of this wealth by the Eye.

The man laughed hoarsely inside his helmet. "Listen, McQuade," he said flatly, "These here stones ain't even chicken feed for the boss. Only reason I'm taking you to him is I think he might be able to use you. You stick with him, and in a week or so you can retire for life. He's going to make us all millionaires!"

There was a gloating and hero-worship in the man's voice that made Wentworth's eyes tighten behind the screen of the spectacles. But more than that was the ominous knowledge that, unless he could succeed in the incredibly one-sided struggle that lay ahead, the man's words were not overly exaggerated. The Terror could at least make himself a millionaire; how his men fared would be a different proposition.

With that thought heavy in his mind, Wentworth for the first time came face to face with the Terror. The man, with his hideously designed helmet, stood with folded arms, legs straddled strongly, atop one of the trucks between two great ray-lights.

The truck was stationary before a massive bank and, before it, the bodies of policemen, and others in civilian clothing—who must have been guardsmen to judge from their rifles—showed how bravely the men had fought to defend it. Probably, a single sweep of the ray had sufficed to blot them out. All about was death and desolation and, in its midst, stood this calm figure in polished armor, motionless and silent as Wentworth was brought to face him.

Once more, anger at this slaughter was strangling Wentworth, so that it was an almost insupportable task to keep the hatred out of his face. He stood mute, while the armored man beside him spoke.

"This here is Blinky McQuade, chief," the man said humbly. "He can make a crib sit up and say 'uncle.' He opened the cardboard boxes full of jewelry. He opened a can down the street, and I sort of promised you'd let him keep some."

The Terror moved one arm in a heavy gesture. "Keep the trinkets, half to each of you," came the voice, heavy, guttural, from beneath the Terror's helmet. "See that McQuade reports to headquarters. You are responsible." Once more, the deliberate movement of the arm—this time in dismissal—and Wentworth forced himself to babble thanks.

The armored man was ecstatic. "Trinkets? He calls them trinkets! Two hundred grand!" he chortled. "I told you he was a right guy. Listen, punk, you stick close to me. We're pulling out of here in about fifteen minutes, and you heard him say I was responsible. The Eye likes guys to obey orders. If they don't…" The man's voice trailed off. "Come on," he ordered roughly.

WENTWORTH SAW that, all along the street, men in armor were drawing closer to the trucks at the crest. There were ten or twelve of them, in addition to those who drove the four trucks and handled the rays. Behind each of the armored figures, trailed one or two men in convict garb. If the other hundreds of looting convicts noticed, they paid no heed. One had smashed his way into a liquor store, and drunken shouts already were rising.

For a moment, Wentworth wavered in his purpose. Once the Terror had left, it would be easy to organize an attack that would wipe out these criminals. If left to their own inclinations, they would riot through the streets, looting and thieving—killing those who tried to stop them, until help came from outside.

He slipped away from his guard and found a telephone. Almost with a shock, he heard the operator's voice over the wire. It had seemed to him that everyone in the city must be dead, except for the vultures the Terror loosed.

Wentworth whispered rapidly, "For God's sake, get a call through to some other town, and call out soldiers," he said. "The leaders are going to clear out in a few minutes, and there'll be only the escaped convicts from Conestoga to deal with."

The girl's voice was shaken from its mechanical calm. "We've already done that, sir," she said. "I hope to Heaven they come soon!"

Wentworth spun from the phone and, seconds later, the armored figure of his guardian showed in the doorway. "What the hell you trying to do, McQuade!" he roared.

Wentworth shrugged and went toward him amiably. "Just seeing what I can find," he said placatingly. "Ain't no harm looking!"

A few minutes later, with two score other men, he was herded into a public garage. The attendants lay dead upon the floor, and a group of handsome cars had been filled with gasoline and made ready for the departure. Also, there were piles of men's clothing. Wentworth was curtly bade to discard his convict's garb.

As groups of men finished their dressing, they were assigned to cars, each under one of the armored men, stripped now like the convicts. As fast as a car was filled, it whipped out of the garage and vanished. Wentworth was stuffed into the third, to go with four other men—all of them with their pockets loaded with loot.

THE CAR tore along unfamiliar roads. The sun had plunged into a cloud-bank, and coldness crept into the car. They saw no other carloads of the Terror's men, even though, later on, traffic began to show.

It seemed strange to Wentworth to see people going about

the ordinary routine of their lives when, so few miles away, such slaughter had taken place. Momentarily, he expected to run up against a police barricade. The disaster at Conestoga and Catskills undoubtedly was widely known by now. But whoever had mapped their course knew his business. They saw only one motorcycle policeman, at a distance, and he gave them no more than a glance.

One of the men in the car with Wentworth was a safe-cracker who knew Blinky McQuade's reputation. He complained that he had not heard of McQuade's arrival at Conestoga. The man was drinking and noisy, and his remarks began to worry Wentworth.

Another matter was eating at his mind, also—he must reach the Terror's headquarters and he doubted that the Terror would reveal its location to the convicts he had recruited. More likely, the men would be sent to some separate concentration place and left there until needed. If they were discovered, then, the Terror would lose only man-power which could be replaced at any convenient prison. Perhaps, if the leader himself knew the location of the headquarters, Wentworth might find a way....

Wentworth abruptly whirled and slammed his fist against the jaw of the crook who had been jeering at him.

"Keep your trap shut!" he said violently. "Who the hell cares whether you heard I was at Conestoga or not? I ain't wanting to talk about it, but if you want to know the truth, I got crossed up in Schermerhorn. A fool doctor hired me to crack a crib in some laboratories there and steal some papers. He was willing to pay plenty so, when I got hold of these papers, I held out on the guy. He got the papers while I was sleeping off a jag and turned me into the cops. They laughed like hell at what I told them."

The leader of the group was twisted about in his seat, staring at Wentworth. "What was the papers about?" he demanded.

Wentworth narrowed his eyes, frowning over the heavy spectacles. "I ain't wanting to talk in front of these others," he said, confidentially, "but I don't mind telling you. Maybe you can guess what they was about. It ain't hard."

The leader said, "Schermerhorn, huh?"

Wentworth nodded his head, "Schermerhorn."

Nothing more was said, but, a half dozen times during the long grind over doubling back-roads, the leader turned about to peer at Wentworth. It was past noon when, finally, the car pulled to a halt in front of a barn-like farmhouse.

Instantly, the car was whisked away into a near-by cow-barn, and Wentworth found that three groups had arrived ahead of them. It took only a glance to prove to him that he had guessed entirely right about the arrangements of the Terror. There was nothing here even faintly resembling a ray-machine or the headquarters of the Terror, himself.

WITHIN A few minutes after their arrival, the leader, a lean-jawed, Latin with the cold eyes of a snake, led him aside. "Spill it," he ordered curtly.

Wentworth grinned up at him crookedly. "Those papers were in the International Laboratories in the safe of a guy named Holtz what got bumped off later on."

"What happened to the papers?" the man demanded.

"The doc that hired me sneaked them off me, and I don't know his name. But he didn't get the copies."

A gun bounced into the man's hand. "I'll take those copies," he said flatly.

Wentworth cringed back from the threat of the weapon. "Aw, listen," he said, "how the hell do you think I'd have the papers when I just got out of Conestoga? I got them papers cached away in Schermerhorn, and listen…" He straightened a little, and thrust his jaw out. "They ain't but one guy I'll tell about them, see? They ought to be worth something to the Eye. A newspaperman came to see me in jail, and he let on about some kind of ray this guy, Holtz, was working on. A ray that killed people—like the Eye does." He feigned slyness.

The leader eyed him sourly through a long minute, but finally pocketed the gun again. "If this is a stall," he said raspingly, "I wouldn't like to be in your shoes when you come up against the Eye. Get me?"

Wentworth spread out his hands, palm up. "Geez, you think I ain't afraid of the Eye? What the hell good would it do me to lie?"

The man grunted, spun on his heel and stalked away. Wentworth found food and, later on, sought out a bed. He was exhausted, physically and emotionally, and compelled himself to sleep.

He had played what cards he held. If they were not good enough, he must find another way to locate the headquarters of the Terror. Once there, he would figure the next step in the battle. He did not attempt to hide from himself the fact that, when he came to the headquarters, he was walking into deadly peril. His life would be instantly forfeit, if his lie should be detected or his false identity pierced. But Wentworth was strangely buoyant, as he calmed his mind for sleep. He might be within a few hours of success and destruction of this whole damnable conspiracy!

He awoke sharply, with a feeling of imminent peril. He knew, at once, that there were men in the room where he slept, but he gave no sign. He lay quietly until his wrists were seized and handcuffs snapped home on his wrists. He started up then, to gaze into the muzzle of a revolver held by the leader to whom he had told his story. The man wore a twisted, ugly grin.

"All right, McQuade," he said grimly. "You're going to get to see the Eye, but you ain't going to like what you see. The Eye says you're a damned liar and the only reason you're going to see him is on account of he wants to look at you before he settles your hash, *personally!*"

The man leaned over, his sallow face triumphant. "You know what happens to the guys the Eye don't like? Yeah, I thought so. He kills them slow, with a little ray—like he did that guy at Conestoga. All right, take the rat downstairs, boys!"

## CHAPTER 10
## PRISONER OF FURY

IT WAS no part of Wentworth's plan to avoid being taken to the Terror's headquarters, even though he went in imminent peril of his life. He made only Blinky McQuade's whining protests against the handcuffs, as the men hustled him to an automobile. They chained his ankles, so that he was forced to lie on the floor of the tonneau, his feet higher than his head. Afterwards, the leader got behind the wheel and, alone, drove off with Wentworth.

The night was black, moonless and, because of his awkward position, Wentworth could guess little about their course. The rough roads gave place to smooth; no towns were passed and, after two hours' driving, once more they jounced over unpaved highways. Finally, the car stopped, but Wentworth was not released. He heard the voices of two men. The driver who presently started the car again was not the same one as before. Another hour of driving followed. Plainly, the Terror did not trust even his leaders to know the location of his headquarters!

When the car stopped, Wentworth saw that the new driver was Monk Burton, who first had spotted him among the convicts. "Hell, Blinky," he said harshly, "and I always figured you was smart!"

Wentworth squinted. "Can't see a damned thing without my specs," he muttered.

Burton laughed hoarsely. "What the hell do you care? You won't have no use for your eyes soon. Lucky for you the Eye went out on a job. He'll tend to you when he gets back!"

Wentworth peered about him and discovered what was plainly an Adirondacks log camp, but he had small opportunity to observe it. He was thrust down crude stairs into a cellar beneath the largest cabin. Burton held a powerful torch's beam upon him, gripping a gun in his left hand.

"Stick out your wrists," he ordered roughly.

Wentworth obeyed, and Burton inspected the handcuffs carefully. Without warning, he struck Wentworth's jaw with the flat of the automatic. The pain was dazzling and, for a few seconds, Wentworth's senses reeled… When he recovered full consciousness, his ankle chains had once more been fastened above his head—this time to a beam so that his feet swung three feet above the floor. His entire weight rested practically on his shoulder blades. And Burton was gone.

A bitter oath leaped to Wentworth's lips, as he realized the helplessness of his position. He had been taken prisoner many times, but never, he realized, had he been more helpless. The handcuffs were a new and powerful type which would have been impossible to pick, even had he possessed an implement. Also, if he had succeeded in freeing his hands, it would have been next to a physical impossibility to reach his ankle chains.

He lay in total darkness on an earthen floor; the cold was eating through his clothing. Wentworth did not despair, yet he could not suppress his bitterness. Success had seemed so near. He had found the Terror's headquarters—but the discovery was completely valueless. For just so soon as the Terror returned, he would be killed!

Damn it, if he could only *see!* He could not even tell how his leg chains were secured, nor how high above was the beam to which they were fastened. If he could reach that beam….

With the strength born of necessity, Wentworth heaved up his body until he could reach his thighs. Gripping the cloth of his trousers with his fingers, he pulled up farther until his shoulders actually swung free of earth. His fingers slipped, and he thumped back jarringly. He rested, tried again. It was two hours before, exhausted in every fiber of his body, Wentworth acknowledged that, until he could see to devise some new method of attack on the problem, he was beaten. If the Terror returned before that time... he was finished.

HE TRIED to drive his mind to fresh plans, but fatigue overcame him. He forced himself to accept the situation, without further futile struggle—to husband his resources and strength against later need. In spite of acute discomfort he dropped into an uneasy sleep.

With the first faint gray light that seeped into the cellar through a narrow window, Wentworth discovered the full hopelessness of his situation. The beams were seven feet above his head. The chain, which bound his feet, was secured to each ankle by a locked bracelet, and the slack of that chain was passed over a beam. Short of pulling down the beam itself, the only way he could free his feet was by forcing open one of the anklets! There was nothing, absolutely nothing, in the basement to help him—not so much as a loose stone.

It was only then that Wentworth admitted himself defeated. Nothing left now, except to wait until he was released temporarily from the chains to be taken to his death....

The sun was strong outside the single narrow window before anyone came near him. Burton brought a bowl of food, and watched him eat, saying nothing to the supposed McQuade's whining complaints and pleas for the easing of his chains. He did bring Wentworth two blankets, then vanished for the entire

day. But at irregular intervals, during that time, a man came down and inspected the chains.

Wentworth decided that, with luck, he might be able to overpower this man. He could spread out his blankets on the floor, wait until the man stepped on one and yank it out from under

## LEGIONS OF THE ACCURSED LIGHT

The Terror cast his lethal stare forth, and those
all around trembled as they saw its effect.

him. If he were agile—*and* lucky!—he might then be able to reach the man before he regained his feet.

But before he tried any such desperate stratagem, he must be sure the man carried the keys—be certain also, that he could devise a way to reach the ankle irons.

THAT NIGHT, when Burton came clumping down the steps with a flashlight, Wentworth had the blankets spread on the floor, but Burton only laughed and stepped carefully clear of them.

"You certainly played yourself for a sap, Blinky," he said. "Know what the Eye did today? He busted Dannemora wide open and turned loose a couple of thousand convicts. They picked Clinton clean as a bone. From what we can figure out, the chief must have taken about five million cash out of the banks. Got hold of five planes, too. They'll come in handy when we tackle New York!"

Wentworth could scarcely force himself to continue the role of Blinky McQuade, so hotly did anger surge through him. In Burton's laconic phrases, Wentworth saw again the destruction of Catskills, many times magnified—hundreds of people massacred so that these fiends could line their pockets. Hourly, the Terror was growing in strength, preparing to attack New York.

Yes, that would be their inevitable goal, as Wentworth had known it would be. Thank heavens, he had sent Nita ahead to warn them. But, even as the thought came to him, he knew the hopelessness of preparations. If the Terror was to be beaten, it must be done here. And he was helpless!

"By the way," Burton said carelessly, as he started for the steps, "the Eye ain't coming back until tomorrow. But, at any rate, you ain't going to die alone. He's sent in some other prisoners—a doc and a couple of dames."

His feet clumped hollowly up the steps and darkness crowded in upon Wentworth—a darkness that seemed to strangle his very soul. Two women had been taken prisoner. God, it couldn't be that Nita had fallen into the fiend's hands!

Good God, the very government of the nation—the civilization of America—hung in the balance! And the Spider, the only man who had penetrated to the heart of the enemy's stronghold, now swung like a trussed chicken from a beam and awaited death....

In the darkness, Wentworth stared toward his suspended feet. But for his prisoned feet, he might escape from this cellar. A thought entered Wentworth's mind and he shuddered away from it, but presently forced his brain coolly back to the idea.

But for his feet, but for one foot—yes, if one of his feet was… removed, the anklet would come loose, the chain could be pulled over the beam. But would he have the strength afterward to fulfill his task? He could not tell, but he had endured many things and survived. If everything else failed, he knew suddenly, he would try… *that way!*

MEMORY OF that project was his first conscious thought in the gray dawn light and, deliberately, he forced himself to search about for the means. It was in this hunt that his eyes fell upon a rusted hook set in a beam. At first glance it seemed hopeless. It was in the seventh beam from the one to which his feet were chained, seven feet above the floor.

The hook was rusted, an old-fashioned meat-spike, and its point was sharp. If he could reach it, wrench it loose from the wood....

Nevertheless, his eyes kept going back to that hook throughout the day, and slowly an idea began to take form.

Terrible longing was in Wentworth to attempt the thing he had visualized. But he dared not try now. Burton might come at any moment. The other guard, too, with his visits that might fall once an hour or only fifteen minutes apart. No, he must work in darkness.

What he could do by daylight, he did. He hunched his body along the ground toward the hook until his chains were stretched to their fullest extent, and he marked where his head came in the dirt. It still lacked four feet of being under the hook. All day long, he worked his body into that position after each visit of the guard, measuring the distance and position of that hook. He closed his eyes and pointed his handcuffed arms— then opened them and corrected the error. He learned to feel the exact tension of muscles which meant that they were leveled at the hook.

When Burton came that night with his budget of news, Wentworth could scarcely wait for him to leave.

"The Eye fooled them completely today," he said. "Everybody was sure he was going to tackle Sing Sing next. But did he do it? Guess again! He went down to Philadelphia and opened up Eastern State Penitentiary like a can of sardines—and didn't use a man of them. While they ran wild, and the police went crazy hunting for them, he slipped, up to the Quaker-American bank and walked out with two and a half million cold. I tell you, Blinky, he's a genius, that's what he is! Too bad you ain't going to be around to see the fun. I got word he's coming back tomorrow sure, and then—New York!"

He plodded up the steps.

EAGERLY, WENTWORTH began the task. He kicked off his shoes and scrubbed around on his shoulders until he could reach them. He pulled out their laces, and, with their help, made sure of the knots he tied in his two blankets, fastening their corners together. Then he wriggled along, until his head rested in the spot he had marked.

He gripped the blankets by their ends and whipped them upward through the darkness toward the hook. They missed and fell back upon his face. They did that again, and ten times thereafter, before they snagged the hook. The instant Wentworth pulled, they came loose again with a small tearing hiss that seemed loud enough to wake the dead.

It was on the seventh cast, afterward, that the blankets caught on the hook, and Wentworth cautiously made it secure with little jerks to impale the thick cloth on the spike. He rested again, clinging to the blanket ends. The crucial part of the battle lay ahead. With less than three inches of play between his wrists, he must contrive to pull himself up those blankets until he could reach the hook.

Wentworth worked the end of one of the blankets under his left arm across his back and up under his right arm so that he lay in it as in a sling. He drew the blankets as tautly together as possible and knotted them. Then he gripped the blanket with

115

his manacled hands, tensed his arms and drew his body upward. When he had lifted as far as possible, he gripped the blanket with his teeth. He swiftly ran his hands upward to a new hold.

His teeth were bleeding at once. After the third time, his jaw was numb, and the hardest part of the climb lay ahead.

He fought frantically to gain a few more inches. All the desperate strength of his will and shoulders went into that final pull... There was a faint ripping sound, a creak—and Wentworth fell.

HOW MANY hours he lay comatose upon the cellar floor, he could not guess—any more than he could estimate the time of his struggle toward the spike. But when, finally, he faintly stirred, he was aware of the cold grayness of dawn creeping once more into the cellar....

Wentworth's heart sprang into his throat. With frantic hands, he began to fumble over the blanket, and a cry he just strangled pressed against his locked teeth. His fingers trembled as, from among the blanket folds, he worked out a piece of rusty iron, six inches long and bent at one end into a hook. The strain of his weight and muscles had accomplished what feeble hands would never have accomplished—had torn the hook from its place.

Wentworth's fingers closed hungrily about it. He was shuddering all over, as he hunched himself over the floor to resume his old position so that Burton and the others would suspect nothing. Rapidly, he untied the blankets. He could not replace the shoes on his feet, but he must invent some excuse for that. The laces... He looked sharply at his legs, tested the keen point with his thumb. Dared he try it now? Which foot....

## CHAPTER 11
## UNDER THE EYE

S LOWLY, WENTWORTH knotted his shoe-laces together to prepare a tourniquet. His face was gray and deep lines gouged about his mouth. It wasn't weakness or faint heart that stopped him, but feet thudding on the floor above—a man's hoarse call. Moments later, the entire camp sprang to life, and there were excited calls, swift goings and comings.

Wentworth strained his ears to catch some hint of the reason. Usually, the camp was not astir until hours later in the day. Was it possible they had been attacked, or... or *had the Eye returned?* He had his answer shortly. Burton came clattering down the steps, a wide grin on his face.

"Get ready to burn, Blinky," he chuckled. "The Eye has come back! You'd better... What the hell have you been doing!"

Burton crossed and stood within a half dozen feet of him, glaring down. "What's the idea of taking off your shoes, punk? Trying to get away, huh? By God, we'll fix that. *Pete!*"

A man answered his call and came stolidly down the steps. Burton spun toward him. "Stay here and watch this mug until the Eye sends for him," he said flatly. "He tried to get away." He turned back, grinning at the despairing Wentworth. "It's only polite to set a death-watch for you, Blinky. I'll be seeing you— but not for long!"

Pete tipped a box against the wall on the far side of the room, without speaking. His eyes rested, almost unblinkingly, on

Wentworth. Above and around them, the camp was violently active, but here in the cellar nothing moved.

Wentworth had hurriedly tucked the spike up his sleeve when Burton entered.

When once more heavy feet thudded down the steps, Wentworth was instantly awake. It took only a glance from under his half-lowered lids to tell him they had come to take him to his death. For the four men wore the armor of the Eye. One change had been wrought in the armor. Now, a replica of the Eye, itself, was in the breast of each man's mail, and they glittered with the hellish green light of death.

When the four stalked toward him, Wentworth jerked up his head from the floor and uttered a wailing cry of fear. He twisted and writhed away from them and babbled out pleas for mercy. No answer came from the men in armor. Two of them knelt and seized his shoulders. The other two seized his ankles, unlocked the chain from one, dragged it over the beam and fastened it again. Then, for the first time in four days, he was on his feet.

His legs had been elevated for so long that they were numb and gave way beneath him. He let them dangle, forced the man to half-carry him up the steps and out into the coldly brilliant sunlight.

The walk across the icy compound was over in a few moments, and Wentworth was hustled into a building whose dimness, after the brilliance outside, was blinding. He heard the heavy shuffle of the metal-clad feet, the clank of the chain about his ankles. Then he was brought up standing, gauntlets gouging into his shoulders. Slowly, the room began to take form. He was in the presence of the Eye!

THE BUILDING was a long, low structure of logs, plainly the eating-hall of a logging camp, at one time. At the far end, a heavy chair stood upon a dais and, before it, there rose the commanding, hateful figure of the Terror. He stood as Wentworth had seen him before the gates of Conestoga, thick, mailed arms folded across his chest, legs straddled and that one fearful eye of the helmet glaring glassily at the prisoners.

Wentworth forced his eyes away from the sinister figure and gazed, hoping against hope, at the others in the hall. Then he dropped his head, almost cried aloud in anguish. His fears were only too well founded. The two women were Nita van Sloan and Sonia Baklanoff!

Wentworth's thoughts winged back over the days since this awful warfare had been launched. His life had become so centered about this figure in steel armor, that, almost, he had ceased to regard the fact that a human being, a man, was inside it. Fumblingly, he recalled his suspicions: that the Terror was either the kidnapped Dr. Canterbury or Luther Gerlaine—perhaps even the supposedly dead Dr. Holtz!

Before this, Wentworth had known criminals to hide behind the mask of apparent death. But it did not matter now. Nothing mattered, except that the man stood before him and that, presently, they all were to die beneath the torturing fire of the death-ray. But it must not be!

He realized Nita was gazing on him. Her eyes widened in recognition, a cry rose to her lips, and died there.

119

Abruptly, the Terror began to speak, rolling out words sonorously from beneath the helmet.

"You four are here to die," he said heavily. "The women are spies who would have betrayed me. You, Tullio, disobeyed orders. McQuade, you are a trickster and not to be trusted. Tullio, first. It will have to be fast. Tonight, we march on New York!"

As abruptly as that, the Terror proclaimed their deaths! At a movement of his hand, two of the armored men thrust Tullio forward and crushed him to his knees. The man was a creature already dead. His face was white, without expression; his eyes dead. The men in armor held him and, once more, Wentworth saw the hateful greenish glow of death kindle in the great eye of the Terror, saw the misty ray stab out and pierce through the man called Tullio.

Pain galvanized him into furious life. Screaming, he sprang against the hands that held him prisoner! His convulsions gave him a strength that was beyond belief. Two more of the armored men sprang forward, one from behind the women, one of those who gripped Wentworth's shoulders. The second man beside Wentworth leaned forward tensely, and Wentworth's eyes, glancing sideways under lowered lids, saw that the helmet had not been fastened securely at the back. There was a narrow gap there, a gap perhaps a half-inch across.

Wentworth's body did not move, but his two hands whipped upward and down in one swift heartbeat of time. In the same instant, he whipped the hooked-spike from his sleeve. As he drove home the spike into that half-inch gap, Wentworth twisted and threw the concentrated strength of shoulders and back into the blow. The man was driven to the floor and a convulsive jerking ran through his limbs. Otherwise, he made no movement at all. But Wentworth did not pause. His movement had been half-masked by the struggling Tullio, and the men who gripped him. The others were staring in fascination at the death throes.

AS HE drove home the spike, Wentworth stooped over and seized the armored figure about the base of the helmet. He could just span it by straining his wrists to the utmost against their manacles, but his swift calculations had not been wrong. With a heave of his powerful shoulders, he lifted the body and, holding it before him, he charged straight at the dais, straight at the awful figure of the Terror!

To do that, he was forced to expose himself to the ray of the Eye, but the Terror did not stand firm. Attempting to dodge, he swayed aside. The ray swung wide and a shout rose fiercely to Wentworth's lips. The heavy body of the guard struck the Terror at the knees, drove his legs out from under him. As he fell, Wentworth leaped to the dais and seized the chair with his manacled hands. With all his strength, he whirled it down at the head of the Terror! The legs shattered, but the helmet held firm. Wentworth aimed more carefully and struck with the corner of the seat, again… again.

The man, Tullio, had struggled to his feet despite the four armored men who had seized upon him. He was dying from the touch of the ray, but dying gloriously. With fantastic strength, he seized the arm of one of the guards, wrenched free and began to whirl on his heels. The guard's feet lifted from the ground, lashed into another of the armored men. Tullio was gaining momentum, beating about him with his human flail.

In a corner, the two women were fighting with the remaining three guards. A mailed fist lifted and fell, and Sonia crumpled to the floor. Desperation put new strength into Wentworth's back. With a final, tremendous effort, he brought down the chair again and heard the dull crunch as the helmet of the Terror shattered. In a trice, Wentworth was on his knees, ripping the fragments away, groping for the throat. No matter if he, himself, died in the next instant, the Terror must be slain! The Terror....

Wentworth started to his feet, staring down into the battered face of—*Monk Burton!* With a curse, he realized the trickery. The Terror had turned over the executions to an underling, a lieutenant, while he himself... Where was the Terror? But Wentworth knew the answer even as he propounded the question to himself. *The Terror had gone to New York!*

"Nita!" his voice rose clearly. "Nita, the Terror has gone to New York! There are planes near here!"

He saw Nita push upward dazedly from the floor, saw her head swing toward him. He repeated the cry. Oh, for a weapon—even for a club with which to fight these men! The chair was shattered. He saw Nita struggle to her feet, stagger toward the door. He heaved up Burton's body and tossed it at the guards, but they avoided his slow throw easily, came on. Nita was in the doorway now, was gone.

## CHAPTER 12
## ON TO NEW YORK

E VEN IN the seeming madness of that attack, Wentworth did not leap blindly. Three men were grouped near one wall, two more at the other and between them was a narrow gap. It was toward that gap that Wentworth apparently was racing. A short distance away, as the men leaped to intercept him, he twitched to the right with an elusiveness that any football back would have envied, and hurled himself against the legs of the man nearest the wall. It was a perfect football takeout. He balled, struck with shoulder and hip. The guard's feet flew out from under him, and Wentworth somersaulted to his feet and streaked for the door.

The chain about his feet was maddening. It shortened his stride by inches and the least awkwardness in handling it would hurl him to the ground. A blow caught him between the shoulders as he ran and sent him staggering. The chain did its work and he spilled heavily. He was up instantly, but partly dazed. He spotted Nita making her reeling way toward a barn to which ran many automobile tracks. She was half-running. If he could only gain her a few moments' respite! His eyes swung frantically about. From the house where he had been held prisoner, a gun spoke and the bullet whimpered perilously close. Then Wentworth saw the woodpile.

He pulled down his head and, bent almost double, raced for the corded wood. Once more the gun spoke, but he paid it no heed. Moments later, he wheeled in behind the woodpile, and a cry of triumph blurted from his lips. He sprang forward and snatched up a double-bitted ax.

From down near the barn, a drum-roll of automatic pistol-fire rang out. God, had Nita walked into a trap? He twisted his head as he ran, saw pistol flame lance out from a narrow window—not toward him, but toward the house! By the heavens, they would yet win clear! Nita had found a gun.

Wentworth had taught Nita how to shoot and she had learned her lesson well. After she had fired, there were no more shots from the house! As Wentworth skated into the entrance of the barn, he threw a single backward glance. The five men in armor were streaming out of the hall toward the main house. Moments later, as he darted to Nita's side, they came out, guns in their hands.

Wentworth's hands closed over Nita's and he rushed out words. "Roll that first car nearly to the door, then knock holes in the gas tanks of all the others. Don't waste bullets on those men in armor. You can't hurt them. Hurry!" He caught up the ax again, spread his feet and whirled the tempered edge against the chain. Two blows sufficed to free one ankle.

He peered through a crack in the wall. No time for more. His hands, caressing the ax, he ran and took up his stand in the shadows beside a small door. The larger doors were shut. Back in the barn, he could hear tinny thuds, as Nita broke open the gasoline tanks.

"You're to keep out of sight, dear," he called softly. "Remember, no matter what happens to me, you must get away and carry the warning. Tell Kirkpatrick everything. He will know how to handle these death-rays."

Nita's voice reached him dimly. "He probably could, but Kirkpatrick isn't in New York. He has disappeared."

Wentworth swore softly and Nita's voice ran on. "Mallion is in charge—a political appointee Kirkpatrick was compelled to place, you remember?"

**WENTWORTH'S JAW** set rigidly and he gripped the ax more firmly. If Kirkpatrick were gone, it meant the Terror was at work. Ah, the Terror was smart! There was no question now of warning. Wentworth must get there himself.

Through the shadows of the barn, Nita was creeping to his side, her task finished. "Get behind something," he ordered softly. "Your bullets may help to slow somebody at the right time...."

Nita said, "Here's a rope."

Wentworth laughed softly. How could he despair, when Nita was beside him, when her courage and her faith never faltered? He told her to hide and she offered a new mode of attack!

"Good," he said, and his voice rang clearer. "Throw it over a beam; make a noose in one end. Fasten the other end to the rear axle of the car. Then get behind the wheel!"

Outside, a gun cracked and the bullet whined through the door, rattled tinnily against a car. Nita sprang back and set about her work. An instant later, a hurricane of lead swept through the opening and Wentworth heard the pound of metal-clad feet, as the men charged. He balanced the ax in his manacled hands, ready to swing.

"Hurry, dear!" he called softly.

Then a shadow fell across the door, one of the armored men charged in and the ax flashed in a vicious arc, its blade striking where helmet and body-mail met. The man screamed terribly. His arms swung convulsively upward and he sprawled sideways, his legs trailing across the doorway. The ax nearly wrenched from Wentworth's hands and, as he jerked at it, the second man charged into him; his gun blasted. Only the fact that he had stumbled over the first man's legs saved Wentworth from the bullet. His ax wrenched free. He sprang backward and struck.

The man glimpsed the ax, cried out hoarsely and tried to stagger back. He flung up an arm and the blade went in under it to the armpit. The man's big body blocked the doorway, as he reeled from the blow. The three behind him thrust at his shoulders, but he was mad with pain. He screamed, whirled and fought to get out into the open air, and Wentworth let him go, sprang back to his guard position beside the door. The man's screams went on and on, but grew rapidly fainter. Wentworth dried his hands on his coat and poised the ax. He heard the motor of the car purr softly to life.

"Ready, Dick?" Nita called softly. "The noose is on the floor!"

Wentworth peered out into the half-darkness of the barn, saw the rope faintly. Nita had made a big noose, spread it on the floor. Wentworth caught it up, enlarged it and stood waiting, well back from the doorway. A fresh rain of bullets. They were advancing again at a run. A body in armor flashed through the opening, but Wentworth waited. The noose must account for at least two… The figure tumbled to the floor, and Wentworth saw that the men had thrust their dead companion ahead of them. In an instant, the light of the doorway was blotted out and, three together, the men crowded through. Wentworth flung the big noose, snatched up his ax.

"Go, Nita!" he shouted.

The gears clashed, the motor drummed, and the heavy car Nita had chosen surged into the broad closed doors. For an instant, they resisted, then the wood splintered under the battering ram of the hood, the noose whipped tight and two of the armored figures were jerked straight upward, screaming. At the same instant, Wentworth leaped forward with the ax. The man dodged, lunged forward and wheeled with his gun coming up. And Wentworth knew that he could not reach that man in time.

Wentworth hurled himself backward, flinging the ax awkwardly toward the last of the men. Overhead, there was a rending crash, a choked, mingled scream, and then a glittering flash. He heard Nita's cry.

"Run, Dick, run! The rope broke!"

Then the two bodies crunched down upon the man with the gun, and, afterward, there was silence.

DUST DANCED lazily in the shaft of sunlight that stabbed through the door. Down the hill, the motor of the car idled, and the wood of the broken door, settling a little, emitted faint popping sounds. There was nothing else. Wentworth pushed heavily to his feet and stood over the crumpled heap of broken armor. Inside, those garments were... dead men. The force of their plunge against the ceiling beams, sufficient to break the rope, followed by their fall to the hard floor, had crushed out their lives.

A hammer of guns from the log house above startled him into movement. He stared uphill and saw that a half-dozen men had scrambled into fragments of armor and were coming to the attack. Swiftly, he stared about him, stooped over the bodies of the dead. An instant later, he straightened with matches in his hand. He flung the lighted book off into the darkness of the barn, caught up one of the armored bodies and flung it toward the car, turned and sprinted past the barn.

"Dick!" Nita cried. "Dick, this way!"

Wentworth flung a word back over his shoulder, a name. "Sonia!"

As he sprinted toward the hall, Sonia staggered out of the doorway. He shouted at her, and the ragged hammer of guns snapped her head around. She began to run, and Wentworth raced to meet her, caught her arm and rushed back to the car. He caught up the armored body, tossed it into the back. He peered back toward the barn. Wouldn't the fire ever catch?

"Dick!" Nita cried urgently. "Not now!"

A moment longer, he hesitated, then he was in the front seat beside Nita. The car rolled forward and, behind them, crimson flame and black smoke thundered in a muffled explosion. When Wentworth stared back, the walls of the tinder-dry barn were afire in a hundred places. Nita's hands on the wheel were light and sure. The car thundered down the rough hill's road, skittered in a sharp turn and straightened out, humming.

Wentworth felt the tension go out of his body, slowly. He

laughed a little. Why, damn it, he had done it! They had escaped from the Terror! Instantly, he frowned. But they hadn't. Some of the Terror's men were destroyed, yes. A place he had used as headquarters was going up in smoke, but the Terror, himself, was ahead, probably already in New York. A skirmish had been won; no more. The main battle lay ahead—the battle which would determine whether crime or law would rule the trembling nation. Wentworth hunched forward in his seat and his eyes gazed sightlessly ahead.

"Phone, Dick?" Nita called.

He nodded stiffly. He would phone, not that it would accomplish much, and then... on to New York! His lips moved and he realized he had spoken aloud. Nita echoed his cry:

*"On to New York!"*

THAT RACE across New York State was a series of nightmare flashes in Wentworth's mind—of deserted and stricken towns, where people fled like starved rabbits at the sound of a motor; of loot-heavy convicts who cheered the car with its armored passenger, hysterically; of futile shouting into telephones into ears that seemed made of stone and connected with the brains of imbeciles.

They stopped first in a garage in an abandoned village, while Wentworth ground off his shackles on a power emery wheel and donned the armor of the dead man. If police were sighted, he would lie prone upon the floor; when looters sprang up in their path, a glimpse of the armor would be enough to open the road. And Wentworth guessed right in donning the armor—they saw no police, but many of the army of crime.

On they rushed.

They had traveled a hundred miles toward New York before Wentworth dared take off the armor—before they found a telephone connected with an exchange that actually functioned. Nevertheless, it took a half hour to get through to Acting Commissioner Mallion in New York City.

"Richard Wentworth speaking," Wentworth said quietly. "I have some terrible news for you, Mr. Mallion. The Terror is going to attack New York. I have reason to think he is already there."

Mallion said, "What Terror? What are you talking about?"

Wentworth began to explain, then, about the rays and the armies of liberated convicts.

Mallion laughed heartily. "We're ready!" he boomed. "Let them come! We'll stuff them back into cells so quick, they'll get dizzy."

Wentworth tried once more to describe the death-ray and what it would do—about the bullet-proof armor the men wore and the fact that only rifle bullets would penetrate it.

"Against the ray, your only effective weapon will be hand grenades or bombs," Wentworth continued.

Mallion interrupted impatiently. "Listen, Wentworth," he said shortly, "this isn't Kirkpatrick you're talking to. You can't order me around. Furthermore, I think you're either drunk or crazy. Whoever heard of such a thing as light killing people?" He laughed hoarsely, and hung up.

Wentworth glared at the telephone and remembered belatedly that he had urged the suppression of all news concerning the ray, itself. He still, on consideration, believed that best. But he had presupposed intelligence in high places and that was a mistake. Should he call the mayor or the governor? Both would be a waste of time. He must get through again to Washington. He glanced at a clock in the drugstore whose booth he was using. God, one o'clock! He was still hours from New York....

It took another hour to get through to the President, but Wentworth had to spare the time. No one else would suffice. While he waited, he bought and used an electric razor, freshened his clothing as best he could, ate hurriedly at the soda fountain. Nita and Sonia joined him there and talked together in hushed, frightened voices. Wentworth had never seen fear rest so heavily upon Nita. In the face of the death of the Terror, she had smiled scornfully. But these miles that they had traveled, through terrorized and desolate country, were making their imprint.

Sonia said, in a strained voice, "I have been loyal to Luther Gerlaine for a long time. I have given him love. But I cannot any longer be quiet. He must be mad—completely. M'sieur Wentworth, this Terror—he is Gerlaine?"

Wentworth eyed her somberly, trying to pierce the veil of her deep eyes. They told him nothing. "Can you lead me to him?" he asked quietly.

Sonia shook her head, shrugged. "He 'ave gone to New York. That is all I know. Once, I work for him. Even here in America, we work together to steal this secret of the ray and sell it. He find it, and then I think he go crazy. He send me away and say he'll kill me if I talk. And he start to use this ray, himself."

Wentworth thanked her quietly. He had to force himself to speak like that, to remain quiescent in his chair while horror breeded in New York. But he was doing his utmost. When he reached the city, he would need his full energies. He waited for the telephone call. He had once more reached his friend in the Department of Justice and arranged for him to get to the President. What he had to say must be for the President's ear alone.

When the phone rang, Wentworth sprang to the booth and that alone showed the fire that was searing his soul. He accounted for himself briefly, told of his efforts with the New York police.

"I believe I have a way to counteract the ray," he said rapidly. "It wouldn't work anywhere except in New York City, but I think it will be effective there. I want at least a hundred planes at Newark airport and Governors Island, all of them loaded with dry ice—yes, dry ice. When the green rays begin the glow, I want these planes to dump their loads of dry ice on the machines. It won't harm any civilians that are left alive, as bombs would; I think it will kill the rays. I know there is no earthly legal or constitutional right to interfere with New York's police affairs, but, sir, this is a national emergency. This is civil war!"

**THERE WAS** something close to buoyancy in Wentworth's step as he strode from the booth again. Nita saw him coming, sprang to her feet and hurried beside him toward the car, with Sonia at her heels.

Wentworth's voice was husky when he spoke. "God grant that we shall always have such a leader in Washington as the President." It was a while before he went on. "Margot Mann and

Horatio Smithers are in Washington, cooperating with federal scientists and with the Chemical Warfare Division of the Army," he said. "If we fail today in New York, perhaps they will discover something that can be used. If there is time...."

After a while, he relieved Nita at the wheel and sent the heavy car roaring through the waning afternoon.

If the President had known how slim was the chance that the dry ice would accomplish the purpose he outlined, would he have been so prompt to second the plan? But Wentworth was sure he would. Anything that bore any slightest hope of success must be tried. Snow would not matter, but God grant that there would be no wind when the Terror launched his attack!

It was four o'clock when finally the heavy car lunged into New York's traffic.

Fifteen minutes had passed when Wentworth wheeled the car into one of the dead-end streets beyond Sutton Place and whirled up toward a pair of mighty steel gates set in a massive wall. The hood was within inches of those gates, when they parted and slid silently into sockets in the wall. An instant later, they had clapped shut again.

From a gun-slitted sentry box, beside the gate, Ram Singh sprang out. A smile showed his white teeth glinting through the thickness of the beard and he swept a low salaam.

Wentworth gestured to him, as Nita and Sonia hurried into Wentworth's mansion. "I am planning things," he said swiftly in Punjabi, "so that the Terror will come here. He may come in. See thou to it that he does not leave, my warrior!"

Ram Singh's hand slid to the heavy-hilted knife at his belt. "On my head be it, master!" he cried.

Wentworth nodded and strode after the women, drew Nita aside. "Sonia is lying," he said quietly.

Nita's eyes rested unwaveringly on his. "She may be," Nita acknowledged, "but it was Gerlaine who seized me at the hotel in Schermerhorn, after you took off in the plane. I went upstairs to get some things, while Margot waited downstairs. Gerlaine was in my room with some men, looking for something. I don't know what."

Wentworth smiled slightly. "That proves my point," he said quietly. "I am leaving in a few moments. I want you to phone our connections at the radio studios and have them say that I have a prisoner—a woman—who can identify the man behind the crushouts at the prisons. You won't say where she is—that won't be necessary. Afterward, you will go into the secret room, off my bathroom, and stay there. Ram Singh will see to it that Sonia stays here, and he will listen on the wires if she telephones."

Nita said, "Very well, Dick. I'm afraid I don't understand."

"Minutes are precious," he said. "The Spider must be ready for battle." His hands rested lightly on her shoulders for a moment, then he was striding away.

He heard Nita cry his name softly, but he did not turn. The elevator dropped him swiftly downward. He touched a hidden lever and, beneath him, the bottom of the shaft slid aside. When the cage stopped, he was in a narrow concrete corridor. He ran through it and, presently, was opening a trapdoor in the floor of a small garage.

The car in it was battered and rusted, but its sides were bullet-proof, as was its glass. Under its hood was a powerful engine with a super-charger. The garage was without windows and, from a floor-trap Wentworth took out make-up materials.

Five minutes later, a hunched figure in a swirling black cape, beaked face hidden beneath the wide brim of a black hat, drove the battered car out of the garage. The Spider was going into battle....

## CHAPTER 13
## DEATH AT DUSK

A ROUND HERALD Square stand three great depart-ment stores and a myriad small shops. When dusk falls, they glitter with lights, red, blue, yellow—and green. Around Herald Square, people swirl by the thousands as the day grows late, massing in and out of the doors; blockading subway stairs, crowding the traffic in the broad streets until its pace is a crawl.

The autos, taxis, buses press nose to tail through the swirls of pedestrians, wedge together in a tangle blocks long.

It was dusk, and the lights began to flash on, red, blue, yellow—and green. The glow of them crept out onto the crowd, into the traffic. A moment ago that bright roadster was yellow—the one with the two girls in it, with the top down. Gay girls in bright berets, laughing, chattering, adding their young, living voices to the tumult of Herald Square. Then the glow touched them....

High and clear above the roar, their young voices rose, screaming. Heads twisted toward them, mouths open. People in other cars stretch their necks to see. They are screaming.

The girl behind the wheel thrusts up with her round young legs—thrusts her body upward and back with her scream. Her head is wrenched back so that the cry comes out hoarsely strained. Her clawing hands grip her clothing and tear. Her breast is white and clean, even in the green glow from the lights. And then it darkens, her face twists horribly and, up from the flesh, little fumes begin to rise—little traces like dark smoke. The flesh wrinkles. It crisps. The scream dies in a rattling little gurgle that no one can hear, and her taut young muscles go lax. She is dead, and the girl beside her is dead.

That was the first of them, but other lights were blinking on now—thousands of lights over thousands of people.

No one is staring now at the car where the girl screamed. In that little circle, where the glow of the light falls, people are all screaming. Their voices soar upward. They fall upon the pavements writhing. A bus driver utters a hoarse cry and jerks to his feet and the ton-heavy vehicle lunges forward into the press of traffic. No one on the bus realizes it. They are screaming, too. Men's, women's, children's voices blurt out frantic cries of pain into the confusion of sound that reaches upward to heaven, without definition, without outline but pitifully clear in meaning: *Death, Death. The Terror has struck New York!*

Thousands on thousands of people screaming, writhing, dying, until the sidewalks are piled high with their convulsed bodies—until the subway stairs are blocked with them. Only the motors of the motionless, patient cars still move, still have meaning, chugging on and on though the hands they served will never touch the wheel again. Distantly, sirens begin their tardy howl. Police coming, ambulances coming. Too late to do anything but bring more victims for the flickering lights. The screams are finished now and the sirens have taken up the paean. One after another, they pour their raucous sound into the dusk-filled air; dozens of them charging in. A police radio car strikes the jam on Sixth Avenue. The men leap out and race for the corner of Thirty-Fourth where bodies crowd the sidewalk. They charge forward, and the green light reaches out and touches them. Another radio car charges in from Seventh Avenue, but there is light there, too—green light—light enough to spare for all who come....

Down Sixth Avenue, clattering over the rough street, trundles a battered and rusty car, driven by a man in a cape with a black hat pulled low over his eyes, the din of sirens in his ears. His lips are drawn in coldly against his teeth, and there is pain in his eyes. Ahead, he can see the flicker of greenish light, but his eyes have seen it before. He whirls into a side street, and slams the car to the curb. He springs to the sidewalk... *the Spider!*

CURSES TREMBLED on Wentworth's lips. This was a thing even he had not foreseen—that the attack should come in this district. What money was there here to tempt the Terror whose loot already is running into the millions? Money in the stores, of course, but there are no armored men about, no looting convicts. The Terror is living up to his name, spreading destruction before him as a warning—killing so that the police will be somewhere else when he strikes his real blow!

In an instant, the ray fell squarely upon Wentworth—and he sprang at its operator!

Wentworth seized two grenades from a box on the floor of the car, wrenched a heavy iron tool from the seat and ran for Broadway. Traffic was at a standstill.

Wentworth ran to a manhole in the middle of Broadway and used the heavy iron tool, wrenched off the cover. He drew the pin of a grenade and tossed it in, slammed down the iron lid and ran on. Before he reached the curb, the grenade's muffled blast cut loose—and the traffic lights went dark; the lights inside stores went dark.

Wentworth ran on. Twice in the next block, he stopped and repeated his work. Men shouted behind him. A traffic policeman's gun blasted lead into the air, and his challenge rang out thickly. Wentworth swore under his breath and ran for Seventh Avenue. When he had done his work there, he doubled around the block.

It was fifteen minutes before Wentworth reached his car again. He wheeled it to the sidewalk, to Broadway and across, up on the sidewalk again. A traffic policeman ran toward him, whistling shrilly. People jumped from his path and shook angry fists. Wentworth pushed on. A mounted policeman drove his horse into the path of the car, but when the machine pushed on and the horn blared suddenly, screamingly, the horse shied from its path.

Finally, Wentworth could take to the street again and turn southward. That was where the real battle would come—was bound to come. Only there would be the millions the Terror would covet.

On a dark side street, Wentworth stopped again and found a

telephone, tried to get through to Mallion, without success. He gave his message finally to a minor official....

"Tell Mallion it was the death-ray that killed the people in Herald Square," he said. "Tell him that's just a feint and that the real attack will be on the downtown banks. Tell him to close off the district with barricades and men, but not to send any police into the section until a lot of airplanes have flown over and until the lights go out. This is the Spider speaking!"

**IT WAS** the best he could do, and he had small hope that Mallion would listen. The Terror had done well to remove Kirkpatrick! Wentworth flung himself back into the car and sent it racing southward.

Even as he sped, his eyes flinched from the skyline of lower Manhattan—the spot where the wealth of a nation was concentrated, of half the world. For those proud silhouettes of buildings, towering upward to the sky, were outlined against a horizon that had turned a deathly, awful *green.*

Wentworth palmed his horn and held it down; he smashed through traffic lights and burned the streets southward. Damn it, where were the planes that had been promised? How long must those rays blaze against the sky before they would begin their work?

God alone knew whether his plan would work, but at least, there was no wind to destroy the effects of the dry ice in the narrow canyons of New York—tons of dry ice, discharging carbon dioxide into the air. Not that it would neutralize the ray. Wentworth had no hope of that, but gasoline engines must have oxygen to continue running! Without the power of his engines, the death-rays could burn only a few minutes, if at all, on battery power. And Wentworth would see that no electricity ran along lower Manhattan!

There were thousands of human beings in the crowded financial district, working in the tall buildings, filling the streets and subways now. Many might be overcome by the carbon dioxide, but it was non-poisonous. If it cleared away in a reasonable time, they would revive. It was doubtful, if, in the open air, they would be overcome at all. But the Terror's men worked beneath helmets whose vents were small at best; they worked in steel, and dry ice was deathly cold. It was a desperate risk. He had known that when he urged its use, and the President had known it, too. The dry ice might kill scores of people—and it might fail! But, unless it proved successful, those same scores of people would become scores of thousands dead!

While thoughts and doubts swirled through Wentworth's mind, he went swiftly about his work, unlocking manholes that led to the electrical arteries of the city, dropping his grenades. Torn and twisted wires short-circuited beneath the city streets, threw whole areas dark, blew safety-fuses in the powerhouses and shut them down. And ever his eyes turned toward those green-slashed southern skies.

It was long before the first of the planes darted overhead and the snowfall of dry ice began. A triangle of ships swept low above the sky-scrapers, dropped their loads and another wedge followed. A green ray lashed up at them, too late. The formation of ships that followed, split and dodged, but one of them shone flashingly for a heartbeat in the midst of that hellish ray. The echo of its crash came dimly to Wentworth's ears.

Now, other rays were licking the sky, making nightmare patterns of light… And the last of the manholes thudded into place and jumped again to the concussion of the bomb. In all the up-thrusting pinnacles of lower Manhattan, not a light showed.

Swiftly then, Wentworth stripped off his cape and the clothing beneath it. From neck to foot, he was arrayed in the armor of the Terror. From the seat, he caught up one of the moon-shaped helmets and drew it down over his head. He slung a bag over his shoulder and stuffed it full of grenades. He had fourteen left. His automatics, he harnessed over his armor, then he climbed again behind the wheel of the car.

Far off to the northward again, sirens were beginning their wail. Probably, Wentworth thought bitterly, someone had complained to Mallion that a vandal was blowing up the electric ducts. It couldn't be that he had taken the Spider's warning! SWIFTLY, HE set the car in motion and raced southward along the dark streets to the east of Broadway. The grand arch of Brooklyn Bridge flashed past overhead and he pushed on. The only illumination in the streets was the headlights of automobiles, streaming northward, and, at sight of them, a hope began to grow in Wentworth's heart. It was unlike the Terror to allow anyone to live within miles of his looting. Were the ray-machines already crippled? He shook his head. It wasn't possible. But they had been diverted to the battle in the skies and so a few lanes of escape were being left open.

Abruptly, the air ahead of him was full of flying white flakes, a deluge of them, coating the street, striking on his windshield and hood and lying there, steaming, throwing off thin white streamers. Dry ice—carbon dioxide! God grant that his stratagem worked!

He raced on, knowing that he went to almost certain death, but unflinching in his determination.

And yet, Wentworth leaned eagerly forward, as he jockeyed through the dark little side alleys of New York's golden isle, heading for the battle of the death-rays. As he pushed on, his headlights began to flick on a continual fall of small white flakes, and the drum of airplane engines filled his ears. The coldness of them struck upward keenly from the streets, and, once or twice, his engine faltered. Beneath the helmet, Wentworth's lips smiled thinly. He switched on the supercharger, bore on toward Broadway.

A dozen feet short of the thoroughfare, he checked the car and sprang to the pavement, jumped hurriedly close to the building. Wentworth had drawn rubbers on over the steel feet of his armor, but, despite that, the coldness penetrated instantly. He peered around the corner. The green death-rays were still at work, but sweeping the skies instead of the streets, fighting the snow of dry ice that was thickening in Broadway and clinging to the steel armor of men.

Everywhere, the white fumes were rising—but the motors of the death-rays roared on. And from the broad doors of one of the city's richest banks, men in armor were carrying bags filled with money.

Wentworth stepped back into the shadows and drew out a

grenade From a truck parked in front of the very bank doors, two broad-beamed rays reached upward into the sky, groping, groping for their prey… striking at the planes.

Wentworth drew the pin and, with steady movements, lobbed the grenade. He saw it tumbling, a black ball in the air, saw it start downward—and ducked to the cover of the stone building. In the narrow street, the blast was deafening. The concussion drummed against Wentworth's ears, and a man began to scream, hoarsely, terribly, without any human quality at all!

Now Wentworth couldn't hear the motor any more. He peered around the corner and saw them dying, saw the green, misty feelers fading into the blackness of the sky, vanishing. He sprang out into the open, ran toward them.

"What happened?" he cried and the sound of his voice beat deafeningly inside the helmet. "The planes are dropping bombs!" he shouted. "The planes are dropping bombs!"

OF THE five men who had been carrying the loot, only two were left on their feet. The grenade had done terrible execution. Wentworth ran on down Broadway, the grenades clanging against his metal-clad hip, his feet numbing with cold. His breath came pantingly, hard-labored, and the inside of his helmet began to coat over. He stumbled, stood with a hand braced against the inside of a building, and pressed a hand to his hammering heart. What the hell… Then he remembered and, remembering, he laughed aloud. The carbon dioxide! If it could strike him so quickly, soon it would strangle off the motors. It must!

He wrenched the helmet from his head and flung it, bounding, rolling, across the street, ran on toward the next ray-machine.

"The planes are dropping bombs!" he cried again.

He yanked out the pin from another grenade, and lobbed it. He slipped and fell and it was a long time before he rose again. The grenade had not flown as true as the other, but one of the giant searchlights was shattered and two men lay in huddled masses on the ground.

Wentworth's chest was laboring in spite of the removal of his helmet. His feet were without feeling, clumping along woodenly on the pavement No matter—he must push on! There still were ray-machines left—a dozen of them.

Wentworth whirled and stared down the canyon of Broadway, and a formless shout rose in his throat. It was dark! The death-rays… were out! Men were shouting, and the planes were still droning overhead, still emptying their cargoes of cold down upon the earth. The sirens were still sounding, nearer now, grinding down between the tall dark buildings.

The battle was won and New York was saved—or, those that were left alive were saved. But it was a trick that could not be worked again. The Terror would fathom the secret, and provide oxygen for his ray-motors. But even so much would not be necessary. If the day were windy, the gas would be blown away. And not every city had the deep canyons of New York that were like boxes to hold the air.

The battle was won, but the Terror lived on. The man lived and the terror that he spread lived, and, unless he were captured….

Dimly, Wentworth remembered that he had set a trap. It was

a long way off, that trap—miles away. Wentworth turned and, in turning, he fell. It was a long time before he got to his feet. He shuffled off the bag of grenades and left them lying there. He left a gun lying in the street and stumbled toward where he had parked his car. He reeled from side to side of the walk and the police cars were drumming down, racing down to meet him. He heard their motors cough and die, as they plunged into the gas-filled area, but they leaped out and came on afoot. Bullets began to whine.

The damn fools ought to have more sense. He didn't want to hurt them, just wanted to go to… the trap. He'd have… have to hurry….

## CHAPTER 14
## BENEATH THE
## TERROR'S HELMET

IT WAS luck that saved Wentworth then—that and the fact the police were ignorant of his plans. He was out on his feet with fatigue and the suffocation of the carbon dioxide. Probably, if the police had surrounded him, he would merely have stared at them and explained fumblingly that he had to go to a trap. He had to travel Broadway for another block before he could reach his car, and the police were almost at the corner he must turn… and the airplanes dumped another load of dry ice.

It filtered down into Broadway, fell with suffocating thickness about the police. It scorched their hands, their upturned, astonished faces. The death-rays had broken their morale and this new substance that looked like snow, but burned their hands... Half their number fell back, and the rest crouched, waiting, peering through the downfall. During those few moments, Wentworth turned the corner and reached his car. He clambered heavily in behind the steering wheel.

He did those things fumblingly, steered erratically backward down the sharp slope away from Broadway.

The cold of the night fanned his face, drove the stagnant air out of his lungs. At the end of a dozen blocks, he could think almost normally again... and he heard sirens begin to take up the chase. He swore raggedly. Not that he could blame the police. They were brave, honest men. Naturally, they mistook him for one of the killers. There was no time to explain, even if he could get rid of the habiliments of the Spider which lay on the floor of the car.

But Wentworth had fully recovered now. He began to throw the gas into the powerful motor. Somehow, the police had managed to sweep the streets clear of traffic. When he had a lead of a dozen blocks, he performed a series of doublings that hopelessly confused the trail. At the first opportunity, he slued to the curb in a dark street, drew cape about him and pulled his hat well down over his eyes. Below the cape, the mail-clad legs of his armor showed, but he would have to risk that. He ducked into a phone booth and called his home.

The bell rang on and on without answer, and fear swelled in Wentworth's breast. The devil—had he delayed too long? Had the Terror fled the scene of battle—or perhaps never been on it—long before his arrival? Just as he was beginning to despair, he heard the click of the receiver being lifted, and Nita's sweet voice came over the wire. But that voice was strained.

"I didn't hear the phone at first, dear," she said. "Yes, everything is perfectly all right. Of course… Why wouldn't it be?"

Wentworth's eyes narrowed. What Nita was saying was absolutely nonsensical, and… Ah, now he caught it, a quick reiterated tapping, as if someone were clicking fingernails against the telephone. That, he realized, was what actually was happening, and there was a rhythm to that tapping. *Morse Code!* Swiftly, he decoded the taps that ran through Nita's talk. "*T-e-r-r-o-r h-e-r-e t-a-k-i-n-g u-s….*"

"I've got to hang up now, dear," Nita said rapidly. "I'll see you later."

**WENTWORTH EXPLODED** from the booth, went to his car in long bounds that totally disregarded the way his cape flapped wildly behind him and exposed his armor. The store clerk gaped at him, foolishly. Wentworth flung behind the wheel and instantly was burning the road northward toward his house. With clear streets, he would have been able to dash to his house within a few minutes, but all the traffic, which had been turned back from the lower town, was cluttering the streets now. Minutes clicked remorselessly past, while Wentworth battled the jams. The Terror would not delay an instant longer than necessary after that phone call. He could count on Nita to slow him as much as possible, to leave some clue to their destination—if she knew it.

Wentworth shook his head angrily. This was the trap he had set, and the Terror had walked into it. But the jaws of the

trap had not been strong
enough to hold. Plainly, the
Terror was in command, or
Nita's conversation over the
phone would not have been
hampered.

At last he was drawing near his goal, but precious minutes
had flown—nine, ten of them. He flung across the line of traffic, raked fenders with a taxi, stalled a truck and slammed into
a cross-street. He leaned forward, his hands white on the steer-
ing-gear. Half across Sutton Place, the car skidded, straightened out lurching—rocketed into the dead-end street that led
to his gates.

Out of a pocket in the gate, Wentworth whipped out a sounding whistle and blew a curious two-toned note, timing it by the
watch upon his wrist. He cut it abruptly, but the gates whipped
open before the charge of his car; slid instantly shut again.
Before the car stopped rolling, Wentworth had flung from the
seat and was racing for his house. The elevator was at the bottom
of the shaft, its door open.

At the sight, a groan welled up from Wentworth's breast.
But he did not check here, sent the cage shooting upward—
burst out into the drawing-room. As he had feared, the place
was empty. In the middle of the floor, a woman's compact had
dropped and spilled powder and rouge dustily upon the rich
Aubusson that covered it. Nita's signal of violence. His eyes
flitted over the room, seeking some clue to the place to which

they had been taken. Nita would leave some signal—if she knew. Some signal....

On the end-table, beside the davenport, stood two glasses in which long drinks obviously had been served. Three straws had been crumpled and dropped on the floor. A fourth had been curved and its opposite ends rested in each of the two glasses.

Wentworth stared at the glasses, through a long minute of absolute blank. Could that foolish thing be a signal...? By heavens, it was! Wentworth skated out into the hallway, jerked open a cupboard and pulled out a telephone book, thumbed rapidly through it. A triumphant cry burst from his lips, but before he dashed from the house, he ran to the rifle-rack and snatched a powerful, high-velocity gun and a box of ammunition.

Two minutes later, he had whirled the car out of the driveway before his house and was racing across town toward the West Side. When he climbed out of the car, he tucked the rifle-butt under his arm and carried the barrel straight down his leg. Then he hurried into a near-by office building.

The lobby was deserted except for a watchman and two elevator boys, and Wentworth realized, with a sense of shock, that it was not yet time to lock the doors of office buildings, barely seven o'clock. He stood before the office directory, then hobbled into the elevator. The boy clanged the gate, and Wentworth was conscious of a curious side-glance. He kept his face muffled between cape and hat. "What floor?" the boy asked.

"Top."

"Everybody's gone up there," the boy volunteered.

Wentworth merely grunted in reply. As a matter of truth, he

was not interested in this building at all, but in the one next to it which was only fourteen stories tall.

As soon as the door clanged, Wentworth ran to the stairs and sprinted down them. His cape billowed behind him like great black wings. He held the rifle at ready across his chest. And there was an angry, merciless set to his jaw. If anyone had seen him then....

MOMENTS LATER, he reached the fiftieth floor and checked beside a window. It shrieked hoarsely, as he raised it, but he did not hesitate. From a pocket of the cape, he whipped out a length of light, powerful silken rope, looped it about a steam pipe and swiftly lowered himself out the window to the roof below. The line was pulled free and recoiled in a half-dozen movements. The rifle at ready again, he raced across the roof. On its far side, the flipped top of a skylight showed illumination from beneath, and that illumination was... Dear God, *it was green!*

Beside the skylight, Wentworth paused for a single instant, staring down into the room below. It was a long, barren room with glistening white counters along its walls; benches littered with chemical paraphernalia. There were many people below. No time to count them, nor to count the enemies in armor who surrounded the prisoners. For from the far end of the room, there glittered the deathly green glow of the Eye of Flame!

With two swift stabs of the rifle-butt, Wentworth crashed the wire-reinforced glass from the frame, poised—and leaped.

Deliberately, as he fell, he threw himself to the floor, tumbled and came up again on his feet, running. He heard men shout, heard a woman's caught scream, but he had eyes only for the figure at the other end of the long laboratory—the figure of the Terror! The green light was shafting from that one evil eye, and he stood tensely beside a large, broad-beamed light, which was trained directly on the prisoners!

"Don't move!" Wentworth shouted. "If one of your five guards so much as moves, Terror, I'll kill you!"

The Terror laughed. "Stand, you fool! Do you think I fear you? One move, and I'll turn this beam on the prisoners—*on Nita van Sloan and Kirkpatrick!*"

Wentworth flung a swift glance toward the prisoners, toward the five armored guards who ringed them, guns in hand.

"Kirkpatrick," he called, "if one of those guards so much as moves a finger, cry out, and I'll kill the Terror!" He faced the man beside the light again. "So I'm a fool?" he said softly. "That is why I know where you are. That is why I have had the place surrounded by the police. You cannot escape, you who call your-self the Eye of Flame. The police are wearing the armor of your men. We killed them all down there in the end of Manhattan!"

Wentworth was inching forward as he talked. He knew that, even if he could bring the rifle into line and fire instantaneously, he probably would not prevent the Terror from throwing the switch of the green light. And that meant death—death for all those huddled prisoners at the other end of the room.

"That's finished, too," he said quietly. "Finding you here was very simple. I heard you had gone to Wentworth's home, and I went there and saw the signal that Miss van Sloan left. Didn't you know she had left a signal—a very clever one? Two glasses with a straw made into a siphon between them, quite obviously meaning that she was being taken to a laboratory. So I looked in the phone books for the International Laboratories here. Simple, isn't it?"

The Terror said harshly, "Stand still. Spider, or I'll let you have this ray in the face!"

"No, Terror," Wentworth whispered back. "No, for if you could, you would have. It is a little defect in your armor, that you cannot turn the helmet separately, but must turn the entire upper half of your body. You know that if you attempt it, I will shoot! And this rifle will penetrate that armor. I brought it along for the express purpose of killing you. But I was telling you why you would never be able to recruit men again.

"The national government at Washington knows who you are!

"Yes, I notified them, when I discovered that you had raided Wentworth's home, after he put that bit on the radio about having a prisoner who could identify you. Sonia said you were Gerlaine, but, if you had been Gerlaine, you would not have troubled to go to Wentworth's House, Terror. Gerlaine knew Sonia's charges were only spite-work, and he was not afraid of them. True, he has had some connection with you. He wants to steal your secret and sell it to some one. As a matter of fact, Terror, Gerlaine is working for you! He thinks he is. He thinks you hired him to steal... *the secret you already possess!*"

**THE TERROR** snarled, and his hand tensed on the lever of the light. Wentworth had advanced a full yard with his fractional movement of his feet. In another few minutes, he could leap—and block the beam with his own body.

"Gerlaine!" Wentworth cried.

"M'sieur Spider!" A man's mocking voice answered him from among the prisoners.

"Gerlaine," said Wentworth, "the reason you gave Sonia into the captivity of the Terror, to be killed, was that you knew she would double-cross you. You brought her to this country to spy on a certain man, and instead, she was deceiving and double-crossing you. Right?"

"You are entirely right, m'sieur."

"Sonia, you fool," said Wentworth, "do you think the Terror intends to let you live? You know too much, and he does not trust you."

"Ah!" choked Sonia, "if I thought that were true!"

"You would testify against him, eh, Sonia?" Wentworth jeered. "So you see, you are finished as the Terror... *Donald Bryan!* Yes, of course, Donald Bryan, head of the International Laboratories, who knew everything that went on within them!"

With the words, Wentworth sprang forward in a great bound which hurled him squarely into the path of the light. As he leaped, the rifle spoke. He had fired from the hip, in mid-air, and the bullet did not speed true. It smacked against the Terror's armor, and his left arm dropped limply, but it was his right that grasped the lever of the light. In that same instant, he switched on the light and whirled to bring the tiny beam of his to bear upon Wentworth's face.

Behind Wentworth, in the same instant, guns began to bang. Lead slammed against his ribs, but the armor protected him. The room was full of the green glare of the light, and Wentworth was conscious of stampeding feet behind him, of women's cries and men's shouts and the sound of blows. But Wentworth was intent on only one thing.

He was running swiftly toward the light, to cover it entirely with his body and, as he ran, he squeezed off two more shots. Those bullets sped true, sped close together, and the Terror's body arched backward, slammed against the wall. Then, slowly, it hunched forward, elbows drew in hard to the side, the knees doubled and it pitched forward on the floor. The two bullets had gone very neatly through the middle of his one eye.

In two more long strides, Wentworth reached the fight and threw off the lever. He whirled, and the rifle in his hand filled the room with the sharp, spiteful crack of its bullets. A clip was exhausted, and he jammed another into the magazine from his pocket, and coolly went on with the execution.

It was not long. Five men in armor were laid on the floor beside their dead master. It was only when that was over that Wentworth discovered Gerlaine. Not all of the enemy bullets had missed. One of them had found its billet in his heart!

WENTWORTH HELD the rifle ready across his chest, and there was a twisted, hard smile on his lips. Margot Mann and Horatio Smithers were two of the prisoners; the aged and broken Dr. Canterbury, who wore a laboratory gown and obviously had been at work here; Kirkpatrick, Sonia… and Nita.

Commissioner Kirkpatrick strode forward, his lean face twisted in a lop-sided smile.

"Spider," he said grimly, "it seems I shall never be done with thanking you for my life. For this night's work, it might be possible to obtain pardons for you from the governor for every crime you've ever done—if you would promise, hereafter, to stay within the law!"

Wentworth smiled slightly. "Only one answer to that, Kirkpatrick," he said flatly. "If I had stayed within the law, you would be dead now."

Horatio Smithers' eyes were alight with admiration. "There's only one man, sir," he cried, "who can come anywhere near you—and that's Richard Wentworth. We were there tonight when the Terror came...."

Wentworth snarled. "Wentworth is a smart man, but he is a fool compared with me! Did Wentworth save you tonight, or did I? Do not mention that man's name to me. Bah!"

He backed toward the door, the rifle still ready. "I'll ask you to stay here ten minutes. It is the least you can do in return for my saving your life."

He backed out and clapped the door shut, smiling as he ran rapidly down the steps. He patted the rifle. He would have to get rid of it now or that clever Kirkpatrick would some day compare the bullets that the Spider had fired with the rifle from Wentworth's house. Too bad. It was a nice gun.

He darted out on the street, past a watchman who stared with bulging eyes; hurried to his car. As he whirled it and headed back across the city, he began to feel the weariness of the hours of struggle, feel a loosening of his body. He drove, and, out of the dead stillness of the night, great slow flakes of snow began to drift downward from the over-laden sky.

By morning, the world would be covered, clean and new. Even the scars that the Terror had left would be white.

**CAPTAIN COMBAT**
- ❏ *NEW:* #1: The Sky Beast of Berlin — $13.95

**CAPTAIN ZERO**
- ❏ #1: City of Deadly Sleep — $13.95
- ❏ #2: The Mark of Zero! — $13.95
- ❏ #3: The Golden Murder Syndicate — $13.95

**OPERATOR 5**
- ❏ #1: The Masked Invasion — $13.95
- ❏ #2: The Invisible Empire — $13.95
- ❏ #3: The Yellow Scourge — $13.95
- ❏ #4: The Melting Death — $13.95
- ❏ #5: Cavern of the Damned — $13.95
- ❏ #6: Master of Broken Men — $13.95
- ❏ #7: Invasion of the Dark Legions — $13.95
- ❏ #8: The Green Death Mists — $13.95
- ❏ #9: Legions of Starvation — $13.95
- ❏ #10: The Red Invader — $13.95
- ❏ #11: The League of War-Monsters — $13.95
- ❏ #12: The Army of the Dead — $13.95
- ❏ #13: March of the Flame Marauders — $13.95
- ❏ #14: Blood Reign of the Dictator — $13.95
- ❏ #15: Invasion of the Yellow Warlords — $13.95
- ❏ #16: Legions of the Death Master — $13.95
- ❏ #17: Hosts of the Flaming Death — $13.95
- ❏ #18: Invasion of the Crimson Death Cult — $13.95
- ❏ #19: Attack of the Blizzard Men — $13.95
- ❏ #20: Scourge of the Invisible Death — $13.95
- ❏ #21: Raiders of the Red Death — $13.95
- ❏ #22: War-Dogs of the Green Destroyer — $13.95
- ❏ #23: Rockets From Hell — $13.95
- ❏ #24: War-Masters from the Orient — $13.95
- ❏ #25: Crime's Reign of Terror — $13.95
- ❏ #26: Death's Ragged Army — $13.95
- ❏ #27: Patriots' Death Battalion — $13.95
- ❏ #28: The Bloody Forty-five Days — $13.95
- ❏ *NEW:* #29: America's Plague Battalions — $13.95

**DUSTY AYRES AND HIS BATTLE BIRDS**
- ❏ #1: Black Lightning! — $13.95
- ❏ #2: Crimson Doom — $13.95
- ❏ #3: The Purple Tornado — $13.95
- ❏ #4: The Screaming Eye — $13.95
- ❏ #5: The Green Thunderbolt — $13.95
- ❏ #6: The Red Destroyer — $13.95
- ❏ #7: The White Death — $13.95
- ❏ #8: The Black Avenger — $13.95
- ❏ #9: The Silver Typhoon — $13.95
- ❏ #10: The Troposphere F-S — $13.95
- ❏ #11: The Blue Cyclone — $13.95
- ❏ #12: The Tesla Raiders — $13.95

**MAVERICKS**
- ❏ #1: Five Against the Law — $12.95
- ❏ #2: Mesquite Manhunters — $12.95
- ❏ #3: Bait for the Lobo Pack — $12.95
- ❏ #4: Doc Grimson's Outlaw Posse — $12.95
- ❏ #5: Charlie Parr's Gunsmoke Cure — $12.95

**THE MYSTERIOUS WU FANG**
- ❏ #1: The Case of the Six Coffins — $12.95
- ❏ #2: The Case of the Scarlet Feather — $12.95
- ❏ #3: The Case of the Yellow Mask — $12.95
- ❏ #4: The Case of the Suicide Tomb — $12.95
- ❏ #5: The Case of the Green Death — $12.95
- ❏ #6: The Case of the Black Lotus — $12.95
- ❏ #7: The Case of the Hidden Scourge — $12.95

**THE SECRET 6**
- ❏ #1: The Red Shadow — $13.95
- ❏ #2: House of Walking Corpses — $13.95
- ❏ #3: The Monster Murders — $13.95
- ❏ #4: The Golden Alligator — $13.95